CW00498928

The Winds

A Nov

Gifford MacShane

Donovan Family Saga

Book 0.5, The Prequel

Copyright

THE WINDS OF MORNING
First Print Edition: March 2024
Copyright © 2020 by Gifford MacShane
All rights reserved.

§

Cover photo courtesy of SarahRichterArt via Pixabay
Cover design by Gifford MacShane

§

ISBN: 9798224859627
Copyright Registration #: 1-9899544982

§

Publisher: Gifford MacShane
Website: https://giffordmacshane.com
Contact: giffmacshane@gmail.com

Works by Gifford MacShane

The Donovan Family Saga

§

The Winds of Morning, Book 0.5, The Prequel
A young woman's desperate attempt to save her family
during the Great Irish Potato Famine.

§

Whispers in the Canyon, Book 1
A valiant young woman, haunted by abuse,
must learn to trust the man who killed her brother.

§

The Woodsman's Rose, Book 2
When a friendship is shattered,
can a fragile young woman with the gift of insight heal the rift?

§

Rainbow Man, Book 3
He'd follow her anywhere, regardless of danger,
but will her recklessness lead to their doom?

§

Without the Thunder, Book 4
An outcast Society belle falls in love with a Navajo man;
can they defeat the woman who's driven to destroy their happiness?

Dedication

For Pat-Mike, Mary, & Nell;
for the many others who survived;
and for all those who did not.

Chapter 1

LATE SUMMER, 1848

The afternoon sun played against the waves of the River Shannon, turning them silver, making them glint like thousands of small fish leaping joyfully upstream to spawn. The banks were lushly green, the sky brilliantly blue. High white clouds, soft as cottongrass tufts, tumbled away to the east.

A girl stood on the western bank, her hair glittering in the late summer sun. The breeze lifted it, teased it, made it fly around her head like a bright red halo—unkempt, untamed, yet somehow holy.

Brushing the wisps of hair away, she stared into the river. Her dress hung upon her in rags. She was thin—so thin the sapling behind her threw a greater shadow. She had no stockings, no shoes, no shawl or kerchief to protect her against a day that was growing cool. And she had no hope.

She was beyond despair. Beyond prayer. And so far beyond the tenets of her childhood that she'd decided to offer her body to the first man with the price of a loaf of bread. At that moment, a voice behind her spoke.

"*Colleen bawn.*"

Molly looked around, saw a man with dark hair and dark eyes, clean-shaven and well dressed. Her relief at his appearance was quickly eclipsed by shame. She could not speak.

"*Colleen bawn,*" he murmured in a smooth baritone as he extended his hand. "Come and walk a little ways." She took his hand without conscious decision, and turned away from the river.

1

She walked slowly, in time with his steps. He seemed lost in thought and she did not know where they were going, or how she should ask for payment.

She stopped at last and he looked over at her. "I must have bread, sir."

"I am sorry, *colleen*, I did not hear you."

"I will give you my body, sir, but please... I must have the bread first."

"The bread? Are you hungry, lass?" He shook his head forcefully, raised a hand to rub his brow. *They are all hungry.*

"No. Yes. No, 'tis not for me." She twisted away, ready to run. If he did not want her, why had he spoken? Or would he take her and then not pay? But she must have food. She turned back to him, shoulders slouching, fingers laced tightly together. "Please, sir. Just a single loaf I need. For my brothers."

"I see." Taking a pipe out of his pocket, he tapped tobacco into it. "And how many brothers have you?"

"Two, sir." She did not see why it mattered, but she would answer all his questions if he would only give her bread.

"And where are they, *colleen*?"

"At the croft. I mean the cottage. It's... it's not much of a cottage, really... but..."

"I see." The man stared at his pipe before he lit it. "All right, *colleen*, suppose you come with me. We will get you bread. Then I will go with you to the cottage and afterwards, you will come with me again."

"Yes, sir." She straightened up once more. He might think he needed to go with her, but she would have returned to him. "Thank you, sir."

He held his hand out again and, like a child, she grasped it tightly. He led her to the public house and bade her sit on the bench outside while he went in. Her taut body relaxed only slightly when he came out carrying a fairly large sack.

She could see two loaves of bread in it, but dared not hope they were both for her. It was all she could do to keep from asking, from begging. Nor could she tell him that the smell of his pipe—the heavenly smell of tobacco—was making her stomach ache from hunger. She pointed out the way, then trotted along beside him saying anything that came to mind to keep from begging for that second loaf.

She told him a tale of tragedy—of how her mother and father had died of starvation, slowly and horribly, her father eating nothing at the end, so that his children might live. How she had taken her father's place in the public works, because she was the eldest child and her brothers too weak from the fever. "I work outside, breaking rocks for the roads because the workhouses... they wouldn't let me out at night. I must care for my family. I am all they have left, and I will break rocks forever if I have to. Yet fifteen hours a day will not buy even a loaf of bread."

Her voice broke when she spoke again of her mother. It had been a week since her death, and she had not had the price of a proper coffin. Her mother had been placed in a mass grave with the others who had died that day. The priest had said some words at the gravesite, but her mother's name had not been mentioned, for there were too many to name, and too many whose names were not even known.

"But I have my brothers still to care for. And that is why..."

"Aye," he said, interrupting her gently. They went the last few steps in silence.

The cottage was indeed a ruin. Its walls were blackened with mildew, its thatched roof half undone. She entered first, both of them stooping low to get through the opening that served as the door. The smell—a mixture of mold, must, human excrement, and the sweetly sour smell of blood—made the gentleman gag. Molly paid it no mind. Her brothers lay on the dirt floor on thin beds of rags, the blankets covering them almost transparent. The younger had gleaming dark eyes and a ghostly smile for her. The elder lay motionless, his breath coming in small, ragged moans, his eyes half-open and unaware of their presence. His limbs were but sticks with flesh hung loosely from them, his belly swollen in a tragic parody of pregnancy.

Silently, she accepted the sack of provisions the man held out to her. Though her lips moved, no words came.

"I will wait outside," he said. "Make no rush. There is time enough."

"Thank you, sir."

He wasn't out the door before she was digging into the sack. It was much heavier than she'd expected. Under the bread was a wedge of cheese and a bottle of brandy. And wrapped in straw against breakage, were three hard-cooked eggs and a small crock of butter.

"Oh, Johnny dear, look," she breathed, waving the cheese under her little brother's nose. "We've cheese! and eggs, and even butter! Even butter for our bread! It must be a miracle!"

"Let me see, let me see!" He dipped a skinny finger into the butter and sucked it off with a moan of pleasure. "Oh, Molly, nothin' ever tasted so good. Give some to Willie, too."

But the other boy lay unresponsive still.

"Nay, I'll give him some brandy first. 'Twill make him feel better. And then later he will eat." She lifted William's head gently and, holding the bottle to his lips, poured a few drops into his mouth. He swallowed convulsively and she poured another few drops. He looked up at her finally, his lips twitching into a smile.

"There," she said, "you'll have more in a bit. Right now it's time to get you cleaned up." Quickly but gently she washed him, stripping the dirty rags from beneath him and replacing them with clean as she went. The dirty ones went into a pile outside the door; she would wash them later for the morning. She glanced around as she stepped outside, but did not see her benefactor. No matter. She would find him again. The village was not so large that he could get lost in it. She stepped back in to wash her hands in an old china bowl, drying them on her skirt.

4

Tearing the bread into small hunks, she dipped them into the butter, for there was no knife left anymore. The softer middle pieces she gave to Johnny as they were easy to chew. Besides, she had a liking for the crispness of the crusts herself. A few pieces she soaked thoroughly in the brandy for William. He was too weak to chew, but she made the bits small enough and wet enough to melt in his mouth. They finished the first loaf, along with the butter, and then she shared the cheese with Johnny, the sharp tang of it like heaven in her mouth. She closed her eyes and held back a sigh of pleasure.

"Oh, I'm stuffed," Johnny sighed. "'Tis wonderful!"

"'Tis good at that," she agreed, wrapping the eggs carefully in the straw and storing them with the second loaf for the morrow. "Now you have some of this brandy and you'll sleep well tonight. And you, William, some for you, as well. After a good rest, you'll both have an egg in the morning. But I must return this crock. To sleep quickly, both of you, and I'll be back in a bit."

Obediently they closed their eyes, and she watched them fondly for a minute. Beneath her breath there was a fervent prayer. *God in heaven, thank you for this day. Thank you for this miracle. I almost thought... No, I knew you would answer my prayers. Dear God, let them live—let them live one more day.* She bowed her head. *God, forgive me. Do not hold my sins against them. Let them live for one more day.*

Chapter 2

JOHN PATRICK DONOVAN stalked away from the cottage, his hands fisted. He'd watched the girl standing there by the river for some time, and had seen the change in her. Seen the slouch of desperation and the slow straightening which comes with decision. And the longer he'd watched, the more sure he was that she would throw herself into the river and let it take her. He could not stand by and watch her die. Not all the pain and suffering and grief he had seen in his own land would let him watch her die.

He understood now that she had not meant to kill herself, that her hard-won decision was to prostitution as a means of feeding her brothers. He could not blame her—he had seen too much. But he could not let her sin.

He knew without asking that she was Catholic. Those of her class always were. He'd been raised Catholic as well. His mother's family were Anglican, but she had converted to the Roman church in order to marry his father. And though his father was dead before he was born, his mother had kept her new faith and raised him as she had promised. It struck him suddenly that had his father lived, he too might be numbered among the starving. A cold wave of nausea gripped him to think of his mother in this girl's place.

He was halfway to the village center when his steps slowed and he muttered angrily to himself. "And where are you going? What are you running from? Have you not seen this before? Have you not been seeing this for the whole time since you left home? Where can you go? How can you run from this?"

He'd journeyed from the city of Wexford on the east coast, where his family owned a shop on the waterfront, ships' chandlers that provided the merchandise needed by sailors for their journeys: blankets and sailbags, iron kettles, corned beef and salt cod, wheat flour, oats and porter. When they had not received an expected shipment of oats from County Clare, his cousin had written to the landowner for explanation, but received no reply. So the family had despatched John Patrick for the purpose of transporting the goods himself.

He had seen so many tragedies—so many families on his way, in just the same condition as these children. He'd arrived in County Clare in a haze of disbelief, only to find that his landowner had fled the country, leaving his granary fully stocked and solidly locked.

"And what makes it worse today?" He stopped and slowly turned himself around, took a long pull on his pipe without realizing it was unlit, then spat the taste of ashes from his mouth. "What makes it so much worse today?"

That girl...

That girl with her fiery hair and her gaunt face was emblazoned on his mind. He had felt her fear, her desperation. He could still feel the calluses on her hand, see the dark rings under her eyes, her pale lips and high cheekbones, the freckles across her nose and cheeks. The pride in her carriage.

Now he must do something to save that girl—for himself as much as for her. If he allowed her do as she planned, both of their souls would be in jeopardy, and his the more so, for he was the one with choices. As so often when he was troubled, he heard his mother's soft voice in his ear.

Consider all the consequences, she had taught him as a child. *Then make your plan and act upon it.*

MOLLY WAS WAITING WHEN he returned to the croft. With her hand in his as before, he led her back to the village; she had to trot to keep up with him. She threw little glances in his direction. He was not a big man, in fact not much taller than herself. Not like her Da, who'd been known as the largest man in the county. But his shoulders were broad and his hands dwarfed the pipe he drew on. He was clean and nearly handsome, with a broad brow, long straight nose and very dark eyes. She couldn't decide if they were blue or black. His clothes were clean, too, and fairly new. His breeches were of sueded fawn-colored cloth, his shirt the finest lawn she'd ever seen. His coat was a deep olive green and his vest a plaid wool of fawn, green and gold. And his stockings were finer than any her Mam ever had. She'd seen no such finery for months—not since the Earl had fled to London.

In the village, they stopped by an old iron bench beneath the tree in the center of the square, and he asked her to wait there for a few minutes. She sat and tilted her head against the massive trunk, closed her eyes. The time had come for her to keep her part of the bargain. *Father, forgive me. I know no other way. I cannot let them die.*

"Hello, Molly." A voice interrupted her prayer. Her hand flew to her mouth as she looked up at her parish priest. How did he know? How could he know? She felt her face burning, but she stood and towered over him.

"Come along, lass." She could no more disobey him than she could disobey her own Da, so she followed him to the doors of the church. There she balked.

"Come in, child, come in," Father Boylan urged.

She saw her benefactor waiting inside. "I cannot. Oh, Father... I need..."

"What is it you need? Come in—there is no reason why not."

To disobey meant excommunication. "But... I have no hat. I cannot..."

John Patrick drew a clean handkerchief from his pocket and proffered it to the priest.

"Spread this on your head, child," Father Boylan said. "'Twill serve nicely. And you must come in, else how will you be married?"

"M-mar..." Her eyes fell closed. As she swayed, John Patrick caught her by the shoulders and held her upright.

"Now, now, *colleen*, 'tis surely not so bad a prospect as all that?"

"No, I... I don't know..." she protested weakly, her breath coming in little gasps. What kind of a miracle could this be? How could he want...? She had fervently prayed for a miracle, but now it was upon her, she could only stand in shock.

"Let me do this," he murmured. "'Twill make things right."

She found no words to answer him but his arm stole round her shoulders, half supporting her, and she began to follow the priest up the aisle to the altar.

The church was falling to ruin around them, for the same law that collected the tithe decreed that it be paid to the Anglo church, the wishes of the tithed notwithstanding. It had been three years since any of the parishioners had the means to contribute toward the upkeep of the building.

Father Boylan turned at the altar, but Molly was hanging back and studying her benefactor intently. "Why... why do you want...?"

"I want to take care of you."

"Always?"

"Always."

"And my brothers?"

"Of course."

Silently she studied him, then nodded twice. As tension drained from her body, she followed him willingly to the altar. She listened to the words of a ceremony she had once known by heart and when the priest asked his name, she heard her groom say, "John Patrick Donovan". She tried it on in her mind—it would roll sweetly off her tongue. But when she heard Father Boylan call her "Molly", she stopped him.

"Nay, 'tis Mary. Mary Agnes O'Brien."

John Patrick slipped a signet ring upon her finger when instructed. It hung like a yoke on an ox. She marveled anew at how big his hands were. Shyly, proudly, she gave the required response and received the priest's blessings, then felt her husband's first gentle kiss upon her cheek.

Mary Agnes Donovan. Molly Donovan. The Lord has sent me a miracle this day. There are not so many miracles in this world. I must find a way to be worthy.

She raised her face to her husband's, tears spilling down her cheeks, and was gathered into his arms. Clutching at his coat, she buried her head in his shoulder. He kissed her hair, then stood her upright again.

"Come, my sweet. We've many things to do before we sleep."

Chapter 3

DONOVAN FACED THE PUBLICAN across the bar that doubled as guest register and plastered a pleasant demeanor over his disgust. It had taken him not a single moment earlier in the day to take the measure of this man and, had there been a choice, he'd have gone elsewhere for lodging. But whatever accommodations were once to be had in the village, they'd been reduced to this.

So he smiled politely while his stomach churned with swallowed rage. In this town where nearly every citizen was skeletal in appearance, the publican's girth was obscene. *And not only is he fat, he is equally dirty. I'll vow that his hair has not been washed in a year. Filthy hands—and I've no doubt a filthy mind as well.*

And the bruises on that kitchen lad's arms...

With an effort, he gathered his thoughts. He needed the rooms and anger would gain him nothing.

"This is my wife." He ignored the publican's sly half-smile. "And I shall need another room also, as my kinsmen will be staying with us for a few days."

The publican openly sneered. John Patrick's dark eyes bored into his and he said nothing but accepted money for the room sullenly.

"Which room?" John Patrick asked.

"Which one yer want?"

"Next door would be best."

"Aye, so be it."

"We'll be two or three days more."

The publican offered him change. "Three days paid. When will yer... *kinsmen*... be arrivin'?"

"Around midnight." John Patrick turned to Molly. "Would you rest awhile? Or perhaps... a bath?" He addressed the servant boy who'd been peering curiously at them. "Could you draw a bath for my wife, lad?"

The boy jumped to attention, eying the coins Donovan still held. "Oh, yessir! Right away, sir!"

"Good. We'll be upstairs then. Knock when it's ready, if you would."

"Yessir! Be just a bit, then, sir." And he disappeared through the kitchen door.

MOLLY SAT ON THE EDGE of one of the beds and wanted to bounce like a little girl. But she was a married woman now, so she must not act the baby. But, oh, how long since she'd had a mattress! and a warm blanket to cover herself. Her hands played over the soft wool and she yearned to gather it up in her arms. *This miracle...* She looked up at her protector—her husband—and found him smiling at her.

"Are you tired, *mavourneen*? Well, as soon as your bath is ready, I'll be going to get the cart and fix it up for the boys. I'll come for you, then we'll go and get them together." He pulled his pipe out of his pocket and lit it. "'Twill be an hour, more or less. Will that suit you?"

"Yes," she answered, on the verge of tears again. But she did not cry—she must be a lady. "Thank you."

He touched her cheek. "No need for thanks, Molly *bawn*. 'Tis I should be thanking you." She did not understand, but before she could question him, a sharp rap sounded on the door.

"All ready, sir... lady," the boy piped up. "Bath's all ready now."

He eagerly accepted the pennies John Patrick offered, and led Molly down the hall to the bath room. She walked in uncertainly, saw the metal tub standing on its claw feet in the middle of the room, steam rising from the water.

She was not afraid of water, having learned with her brothers to swim like a fish in the river. She'd heard of tubs, of course, but never before actually seen one. Throughout her life, she had washed in the white china bowl that was the only possession of her mother's she had left. Once there had been a beautiful blue-flowered pitcher to match it, but one of her brothers—or both of them—had broken it accidentally. There'd been no money to replace it.

"Ye lock the door, miss—I mean, mum," the boy advised. "An' ye drape summat o'er the handle there, so's the keyhole's blocked up. Don't want nobody starin' in at ye now, do ye?"

"Oh, no." Would people really...? But he was gone before she could thank him, the door closing hard behind him. She shot the bolt home and slowly approached the tub.

She stared at the water, at the steam, and slowly, hesitantly, dipped her fingers into it. How warm—how delicious! She stripped quickly, remembering at the last minute to throw her tattered apron over the handle to obscure the keyhole, then lifted up her foot and submerged it in the water.

She almost moaned in delight as she sank deeply into the tub. *What a wonderful thing! My skin is tingling—oh, my dear Lord, what a wonderful thing!* She lifted her hair up, draped it over the side of the tub—she'd heard that one could catch the fever going about at night with wet hair. She lay there for several moments, then with the soap the boy had given her slowly, luxuriously, beginning at her feet, she washed every inch of herself. And then lay back again in the water until it began to cool.

Reluctantly she got out of the tub and, even more reluctantly, she put on her only clothing. At least her body was clean, even if her clothes were dirty. She'd never been so clean in her life. Had he offered her the bath so that she would be clean for him? Well, fair enough. He'd kept his part of the bargain, and she would surely keep hers. What would it be like? She very much wanted him to be pleased with her.

She strolled down the hall to the room and was thinking she might lie down for just a bit when she heard footsteps on the stairs. She peeked around the door. She was beginning to expect the deep smile that greeted her—it warmed her inside as the bath had warmed her skin. She was his wife! It was so difficult to believe when he was not with her, so easy when she saw his face again. For the first time in over two years, security sat upon her shoulders like a shawl. A hard core of fear inside her stomach was slowly melting away. She went gladly to meet him.

SHE WAS QUIET AS SHE rode beside him to the croft but whatever her thoughts were, John Patrick did not interrupt them. The night was turning colder, but she seemed not to notice. As he helped her out of the wagon, his hands spanned her waist and he was struck again by the gauntness of her—the frailty belied by the spark in her eyes. She ran inside, leaving him to follow at his own pace. He stopped for a moment to light his pipe and entered to see the elder boy still deeply asleep.

"But I don't believe it!" Johnny was whispering. "And how can ye be married when ye never set eyes upon him before today?"

"Hush!" She shot a look of guilt toward her husband.

He winked at her, then said to the lad, "'Tis true enough. Now the question is whether you care to come and live with us."

"And what choice have I? Do I look able to care for meself?"

"Johnny, hush!" Molly whispered fiercely. "Of course he'll come with us and be glad of the chance." She turned back to the boy and muttered under her breath, "Ungrateful wretch!"

But her brother's eyes glinted with glee. He held her hand tightly against his breast. "And where would I be without ye, darlin' Sis? And when would I ever let ye go wanderin' about alone?" He laughed softly at her. "Ye know ye've no chance o' gettin' rid o' me. But just where is it that we're goin'?"

"Oh, Johnny, you are a wretch!"

"We've rooms at the public house for two or three days," John Patrick said. "Then, God willing, we'll be for Wexford."

"Wexford? Ain't that quite a good ways off? Well, Sissie, if that's what ye've planned, it's fine by me."

John Patrick tapped out his pipe. "All right, lad, I'll take you out first. Molly, run and get a blanket for him, won't you?"

He wrapped the boy snugly and lifted his slight weight up, carried him out to lay him in the thick bed of hay in the cart. Tucked round with more blankets, Johnny stared up at the stars and smiled a crooked little smile but made no comment.

John Patrick returned to the cottage to find Molly trying without success to rouse the elder boy.

"It must be the brandy," she said. "He never sleeps so sound."

"Never mind. We'll take him as he is. Maybe it's better that he sleeps—the ride might make him squeamish."

He carried the frail boy out to the cart and Molly bustled around him, tucking and folding, fluffing the straw up, covering his head with a cowl of blanket. Then she jumped out of the wagon and brushed herself off.

"Ready?" her husband asked.

"Oh, no! I've got to get my things." She disappeared into the hut to emerge with the half-empty sack of victuals, the white bowl and a sledgehammer. He stowed the food under the seat then took the bowl from her.

"This is chipped, Molly. We can get a new one."

"'Twas my mother's."

"Aye." He packed it carefully in the straw, grasped the hammer and held it silently.

"For my work," she told him.

A shudder passed over his body. He put the hammer on the seat of the cart, then put his hands on her shoulders, drawing her close. His voice shook as he said, "There will be no more work, Molly *bawn*. There will be no more rocks to break. You are my wife. I will take care of you." He pulled her close, held her tight. "Molly, sweet Molly," he whispered into her hair, "I will take care of you. There will be no more work."

She clung to him and he did not know if she was shaking, or if his emotion was shaking her. But finally she stood back and said, "Then I shall give it to O'Fagan. He helped me—he helped us... as best he could.

"'Tis a good hammer, and better than his. I'll give it to him."

Chapter 4

THE LIGHTS WERE OUT at the inn by the time they returned, and John Patrick sent Molly up for a candle, begging her to be silent.

"You be still, too, lad." He wagged a finger at Johnny, for the boy had spent hardly a quiet moment on the journey, alternately teasing and charming his sister. "Or you'll be bringing that great greasy pig of a landlord down upon us."

Johnny's bright eyes flashed at him, but he made not a sound as his sister returned and her husband uncovered him. The boy marveled at the gentleness of the big hands that lifted him up, at the strength in the arms that did not appear brawny, and the warmth that seeped through his coat with the faint scent of cedar. He remembered his Mam had said that a good coat could hide a hundred flaws—obviously, it could hide more than that.

Molly gathered up his blankets and they all three crept up the stairs. They left him in the room alone and went down for his brother, who slept deeply throughout. Then John Patrick closed the door firmly behind him, having told them he would tend to his animals. Molly pulled and fussed at his blankets until Johnny rebelled.

"Leave be, woman! 'Tis good enough. In fact, 'tis the best we've had in many a day." His little half-smile appeared. "Your Eastern dandy is quite a one, ain't he?"

"He's no dandy! Our own Da had a coat just like that—and quite as nice, too, when it was new."

"Peace, Molly, I meant no disrespect. But we've not seen the likes of him in these parts for a long while."

"Aye. But you've no call to be making fun of him. If not for him..."

"I know. I'm sorry. I'm truly glad ye found him. Ye need someone to take care of ye."

"And you don't, I suppose? All of fourteen years old you are—and able to do the work of two men every day!"

Her brother turned his face to the wall, but not before the fire of shame stained his cheeks.

"Oh, Johnny dear! 'Tis my turn to be sorry. I know you would if you could."

"Do ye?"

"Yes, my love, my little one." She leaned over to hug him and her tears fell on his forehead. "I'm so sorry. I'm so... so confused." She wiped her cheeks with the backs of her hands. "I cannot believe..."

"I know. It seems too good to be true."

"A miracle. And I'm afraid..."

"Now, Sissie, don't be thinkin' that way." He took her hand in both of his. "Would he be takin' us in if he meant to abandon us? 'Twould be much easier to leave us be. No, he's an honorable man. And he... I think... he loves ye."

"Don't be silly! He met me just today." But her eyes slowly lost their focus, and Johnny made no further comments.

John Patrick returned moments later with his arms full. He gave the bowl and the sack of food to Molly and leaned the sledgehammer up near the door as Molly put the bread out on the battered chest that sat under the window.

"Ah," Johnny said, reaching for the loaf, "must be supper time. And there's eggs there, too, ain't there?"

"'Tis for breakfast," his sister replied, gently swatting his hand away. "You be a good boy and leave it."

"Let him have it," her husband said softly. "There will be more when morning comes."

Johnny tore off a large hunk and stuffed it into his mouth.

18

"Easy, lad." John Patrick took the loaf, broke off a much smaller piece and gave it to the boy. He cracked an egg open, offered another to Molly, but she shook her head. He found the brandy as well as a rude wooden cup, filled it and placed it on the chest within Johnny's reach. He ruffled the lad's black hair. "Drink that up, and then to sleep with you."

"Yessir." He spoke around a mouthful of egg and bread. "G'night, sir."

"Good night, boy. Come now, Molly, let's give this lad some rest."

MOLLY FOLLOWED HIM to their room. It was identical to the room her brothers were in—two single beds of roughhewn wood and cottongrass mattresses. One stood against each long whitewashed wall, with the door and opposite window between. An ancient chest claimed the space beneath the window. The room was reasonably clean, though the white coverlets were dingy and the blankets thin, and a musty smell hung over all. John Patrick closed the door and sat down on a bed.

"Come here, my love." He patted the bed next to him.

She sat, her hands interlinked in her lap. He covered them both with one of his.

"Molly *bawn*, I know this day has been difficult for you. But you must listen to me carefully." She nodded without looking up. "I am not a rich man, Molly." His family's worth would be beyond her comprehension, yet the greatest portion belonged to his grandfather and his uncles, who shared it generously. His own income would not have supported them in the same manner. "I am not rich, but I've enough to provide for you and your brothers. There will be more food in the morning—there will be food every morning, and whenever you are hungry. There will be blankets and coats, and medicine when you need it. You will have everything that you need. You've only to say."

He raised her face to his. "You'll not go hungry any more. Do you understand me?"

"Do you promise?"

"I swear to you, Molly, by all that is holy. I will provide for you, if I must sell my very soul to do it."

"And the boys?"

"And the boys, of course."

She drooped against his shoulder as if her strength had suddenly washed away. His arms went around to cradle her, then one hand crept up to stroke her hair. It was softer than he'd imagined as his fingers buried themselves in it.

"Molly." He didn't want her to sleep; their long, hard day was not yet over. "Molly."

She murmured a response.

"Your brother... William... you know he is... quite sick."

She sighed so deeply it was almost a moan. She pressed her cheek tightly to his shoulder. "He'll die, won't he?"

"Yes, my love," he said as gently as he could. Her hot, silent tears burned though his vest. "Oh, Molly *bawn*, I'm so sorry."

"Will it be soon?"

"I'm afraid so. I shall ask the priest to come in the morning."

He felt her nod against his neck, then heard her fearful whisper, "And Johnny?"

"I think, my love, that it is not too late for Johnny." If only he'd arrived a month ago, he could be sure. "He has not had the flux, has he? Then I believe he may recover. We will pray that he does."

"Yes," she whispered into his chest. "We will pray..." But her tears ran with sorrow for the elder brother, and she had no strength left. It was just a few minutes before she slept in his arms.

He found himself unable to let her go. He leaned on the wall and let her head slip down into the hollow of his shoulder. One of her hands crept up to rest upon his breast, but otherwise she did not stir.

He kissed her forehead, laid his cheek against her hair and held her there until the first dim light of dawn.

He moved cautiously at first, not wanting to wake her, but found he could not stand without lifting her up. Yet even as he lay her down and raised her feet onto the bed, she only stirred slightly. He took the blanket from the other bed to cover her, and crouched beside her to brush the stray tendrils from her face.

My poor girl. How I wish... But there was no sense in wishing. He went to see how her brother had fared through the night, returned immediately and shook her shoulder gently.

"Molly. Molly, wake up." Her eyes half-opened. "Molly *mavourneen*, wake up. You must come now."

Slowly she focused on him. "Is it William?"

"Yes. You must come now."

"Then he is not..."

"Not yet, my love. But you must come."

She stood up quickly. Her face blanched and he caught her before she could fall. She clung to him, her whole body shaking. He helped her to stand upright.

"You must be brave, *colleen*. He will need you to be brave."

She choked back a sob. Her spine straightened—as it had at the river—and he knew she would find the strength she needed. She dashed a hand across her eyes as he moved slightly away from her. She did not waver.

"I will get the priest," he said, touching her cheek. "Be brave, Molly. I know you can."

He left her gathering her courage and ran down the steps three at a time, praying as he went that he would not be too late.

MOLLY WIPED HER HAND across her face once more and, as she entered her brothers' room, she was struck by the smell—no longer pungent and sickly, but pure and sweet as a morning rain. She knew what it meant: the same thing had happened when her Da died.

William's blue eyes were open and focused on her. His hand twitched on the covers and she took it in hers as she sat next to him. She leaned over to kiss his brow, found it cool beneath her lips.

"Willie," she said with a sweet smile, "do you feel better?"

"Aye." His voice was weak, as were his fingers as they squeezed hers. "The pains are gone. The burden is lifted off me chest. 'Tis much better."

"I'm so glad! Ah, Willie..."

"Don't fret, Sissie. No use to fret. Ye've done what could be done, and I thank ye. Is it true what Johnny says? That ye've up and married a stranger?"

"Aye, 'tis true."

"I'm glad, Molly. I'm glad ye'll have someone to look out for ye. Ye've been so good to us."

"Hush! 'Tis nothing you would not have done yourself."

"But I was not able. Ye've done it for us. I love ye, Sissie."

"And I love you, Willie."

"Don't cry, girl. There's a better place for me now. And this will be a better place for ye—with someone who can look after ye. Let me see ye smile, Molly.

"Johnny, make her smile."

She looked over at Johnny, saw that his face was as wet as hers. She fought the tears off, forced a smile to her lips.

"Aye, that's better," said William. "Ye're so pretty when ye smile—ye look so very much like Mam..." His voice trailed off, and Molly was afraid to use hers for fear she would start crying again. So she stroked his hair and watched as his eyes slowly closed.

William roused himself when John Patrick came in with the priest.

"That's him?" he asked in a voice that was almost gone. At her nod, he lifted his head and addressed himself to John Patrick with an effort. "Thank ye, sir... for..." He fell back, his strength gone.

"No need for thanks," Donovan replied, touching Molly's hair. "Come, lass, and let the priest—"

"No." William's voice was weak but insistent, his hand clutching at his sister's. "Stay, Sissie... don't go..."

Molly looked a question at the priest, who was draping a purple stole around his neck. Father Boylan nodded and she soothed her brother's brow.

"I will stay. Don't you fret."

William gave her a smile of such beauty that it made her heart ache.

JOHN PATRICK PICKED up the younger boy and took him out, leaving the door open a crack behind him. He settled Johnny in the other room, then came to stand in the hall. He listened to the priest's voice, the low responses of the dying lad, the final blessings, and then no sound but the weeping of his wife.

He went to her and she turned her face up to him. Willie lay still, his hand limp upon the blanket. John Patrick knelt and bowed his head in prayer. Molly sank against him and his arm went round her waist.

"Oh, Molly, *mavourneen,* I am so sorry." She choked on a sob and he held her more tightly. "Shhh..." He soothed her as he would a child, stroked her soft hair. "Hush, my love, *macushla.* Shhh..."

It was not long before she ceased to cry. She was limp as a rag when he picked her up as he had picked up her younger brother, asked the priest to wait for a minute, and carried her back to their room. He motioned to Johnny for quiet, and she was asleep before her head touched the pillow.

"Is't over then?" the boy whispered.

"Yes, lad. I'm sorry."

"She tried so hard." Tears streaked his face. "'Tis not fair."

"I'm sorry." John Patrick put a hand in the lad's hair, left it there for a moment. "Listen, lad, if I turn you 'round the other way—with your head down there—do you think you could reach the latch?"

"Sure."

John Patrick helped the boy turn himself so that his feet were at the window. "Lock this, then, when I go and let no one in but myself or Father Boylan. No one, you understand?"

"Yes, sir." Johnny frowned as John Patrick lifted Molly's foot and measured it against his forearm.

"No one at all," John Patrick repeated as he left the room. And after he closed the door, he heard the latch click into place behind him.

Chapter 5

IT WAS LESS THAN AN hour later that Johnny began to feel restless. He'd snatched up the bread and the remaining egg when John Patrick had removed him to this room. With great effort, he turned himself around so that he could reach the food on the chest. This time he chewed slowly, savoring every bite and wondering if there were truly a place in the world where people always had enough to eat.

When the food was gone, he spent a while staring out the small window, but the morning was quiet and there was no one about. Those who could work were working. Those who could not had no strength to be walking around in the village. Once in a while he heard the distinctive ring of metal, which told him that the blacksmith was busy at his forge on the far side of the square. Aside from that, it was only the rustle of leaves in the cool breeze and his sister's occasional sigh that broke the silence of the morning.

Such quiet was a stark reminder of how life in this little village had changed over the past three years. Before, there had been a daily hustle and bustle of women in the early morning—a social occasion disguised as marketing, accompanied by the smell of fresh-baked goods, and the squeal of pigs and clucks of chickens to be sold or traded in the square. At noon, the younger boys would run home from the hedge school, shouting for their friends, taunting one another with their feats of prowess, or fighting over a girl. The old women would sit knitting or tatting on the rusted iron benches that surrounded the square, gossiping or telling the tales of days past. Later, the men would gather in the square or at the smithy to argue about the weather or roar with laughter at the latest whispered jibes against the English. And later still, in the soft coolth of evening, they drank and sang the old songs, and made plans for the future of their children.

The old men had died first, and only a half-dozen of the fathers were still alive. The boys who could were working on the road gang. The women were weak—so weak they were unable to bear more children. The younger among them were confined to the workhouse. The old women were gone, too, except for Mother O'Fagan, a white witch said to live on the air she breathed. The chickens and pigs had been eaten these past two years or more. Even the benches were gone, except for the one that ringed the tree in the square. Father Boylan had arranged for them to be sold this past spring, and had spent the proceeds on corn meal and salt cod to feed the most needy of his flock. The food had not gone far, and most of those who had partaken were gone now, too.

Willie had been one of them. Heartsore, Johnny sighed deeply. Willie had been the first of the family to get sick, and the sacrifices his Da had made to keep his eldest son alive had in turn caused his own death. It had become so common a practice that the Church had made an exception to the suicide exclusion, and allowed those who starved themselves to be buried in hallowed ground.

So his Da had died, and then his Mam. He believed that she had died of a broken heart. And now Willie. All that was left was himself and Molly, and she had been working so hard for so long that he had often wondered if she wouldn't just drop dead at her job. He had prayed fervently for her—for her strength. He was afraid to die, and knew she was his only hope.

She lay on the bed across from him. For months there had been a furrow in her brow as she slept, but it was gone now. She seemed at peace. *She looks dead—oh, God help me if she's dead! Don't let her be dead!*

He scrabbled to the edge of the bed, stretched out to touch her but could not reach. He groaned aloud.

"Molly. *Molly!*" Her eyes opened slowly, hazy and heavy with sleep. His breath went out in a puff; he pulled his hand in and was silent. She slept again at once and he berated himself—how foolish to think she would die now, when life was so much better. Would be so much better. And yet he could not help but wonder what her new husband would have done if she in fact died. Would the promise he had made to Molly to take care of her brothers still bind him? Johnny believed that it would—that Donovan was a man who would not go back on his word no matter what the circumstances. And thinking thus, he fell into a reverie about what their new life might be.

He'd no idea how lengthy a journey it would be to Wexford—he only knew it was a long way off. He'd never been to the ocean. He'd never been anywhere except once to the county seat of Clare, some fifteen miles away, with his father to buy some pigs. He'd been amazed at the size and the noise of that city, the voices of the people teeming in the streets. The squeals and baas and clucks of the animals for sale, the neighs of horses and donkeys fighting for supremacy over the creaks of wagons on their way to and fro.

He wondered if Wexford would be the same, and if the ocean would come right up to the houses. If the house were big or small, if the yard would have trees and chickens. If the people would be friendly to a stranger. If he would be able to put his bare feet in the sea and walk along the beach and hear the sea birds cry. He fell asleep and dreamed of the sea birds swooping into the ocean and dropping their catches at his feet—mussels and clams and crabs and even eels, then bread and crocks of butter and jugs of porter. And in his sleep he smiled because his belly was full.

A SINGLE SHARP RAP on the door woke him. Turning around came more easily, but not before the rap came again. "Keep your shirt on. Give a body a chance."

"Open up, lad." Donovan came in loaded down with parcels, not the least of which was another sack of food. He dumped them unceremoniously at the head of Johnny's bed.

The boy turned himself around and grabbed for the victuals; John Patrick's attention was occupied elsewhere. He was looking down at his bride, who was sleeping on her back with one arm over her eyes. *Like a child. Like a beautiful little girl. God grant us such beautiful children.* He stroked her hair but she did not stir. He shook her shoulder gently.

"Molly *bawn*." His voice was full of compassion. "Wake up, *colleen*." He moved her arm away from her eyes and she squinted against the light without opening them. "Wake up, lass. Father Boylan is waiting for us."

Her eyes opened at last, their pale blue depths shiny with tears. He helped her up, held her close for a minute and kissed her forehead.

"The good Father is ready for the service." He reached for the parcels on the bed, handed her two of them. "I bought these for you. I hope they fit."

She stared at him for a moment, then sat up quickly and tore at the wrappings of the first package, eager as a child at Christmas. It was hard and unwieldy and contained a new pair of walking boots. The second was larger, softer, more symmetrical. He watched as she opened it carefully, picking items out one by one—a plain woolen dress, a white linen apron, a muslin chemise, and a pair of lisle stockings. And at the bottom, a starched white bonnet with eyelet trim. She gathered them to her bosom and looked up at him, her gratitude finding no words.

He touched her face—that look was worth the trouble he'd been through. He had found no clothing for her in this village, or even in the next, and had gone to Clare and back to procure these. The apron he'd purchased from a peddler he'd passed along the way. The dress would be too large, he was sure, but the apron would hold it in against her. The bonnet was better suited to high summer, but was the only one available at any price, and she needed it for church. And the stockings—well, he'd annoyed the mistress of the shop no end until he had found a pair that he thought would be both presentable and serviceable. She had tried to talk him into a prettier, flimsier pair but he was buying not only for today, but for the journey that lay ahead.

"You've just time to change," he told his wife. "We—"

"Sir." It was Johnny's voice piping up, interrupting him. He turned to the lad and saw a chunk of bread already in his hand. The boy smiled bashfully at him, "Sir... I'm sorry, sir, but... I've forgotten yer name."

"John Patrick."

"That's a mouthful, ain't it? I don't suppose there's anything shorter-like...?"

He looked at the lad for a moment with no expression, saw that Johnny was afraid he'd gone too far. Then John Patrick gave a snort of laughter. He saw the charming, lop-sided smile appear again on the boy's face as he answered, "The nieces call me 'Uncle Pat'. Seems they haven't many brains, either."

The boy laughed outright, accepting the insult with good grace. "Well, Pat, I'm just wonderin' if there's not somethin' in one o' them parcels for me." He held up an arm from which his nightshirt hung in tatters. "Seems I could use a little somethin' new." He looked away, mildly embarrassed by his brashness.

John Patrick lit his pipe. "There's a new nightshirt for you. And some socks and slippers. And if you'll finish digging in that sack, you'll find a jar of honey at the bottom."

"Really? Oh my!" He stuck his arm clear down into the bag, unerringly finding the honey. He lifted the lid and stuck his crust of bread deep into the jar. It came up glistening and dripping bright amber beads of sweetness and he stuffed the whole thing into his mouth. His thanks were an unintelligible gurgle and John Patrick laughed at him again.

"Glutton!" he admonished, then added seriously, "Don't eat it all at once, lad, or you'll have a serious bout of colic."

Johnny nodded enthusiastically, still munching, then pointed. John Patrick turned, saw that Molly had somehow managed to don her new clothes during their conversation.

Her smile spoke volumes to him. She was still too thin, and her eyes were still shadowed with exhaustion, but they were shining like the evening star. Her fiery hair was tamed by the bonnet, and with the two inches the new shoes gave her, she was as tall as he. She stroked the linen apron again and again. His heart leapt in his breast—she was a woman in these clothes, not a girl, and he loved her more than he had ever believed it possible to love.

"One moment..." Searching through the remaining parcels, he found the smallest one and opened it, then drew a black shawl round her shoulders. She rubbed her cheek against it, and then her eyes met his, glistening with thanks.

"We must go, my love," he said. She held out her hand and he tucked it under his arm. "Mind you latch the door, lad."

JOHNNY DIPPED ANOTHER crust into the honey, then forced himself to put the lid on the pot. Three pieces were almost enough to fill his stomach, and he did not want to be sick. *But oh! the taste of it! So sweet and smooth.'Tis better than cakes and ale. And how long it's been since cakes and ale...*

He remembered to latch the door, then found himself drawn to the sack of food again, through simple curiosity. More bread, some dried currants, sausages and smoked fish, and a bag of gritty meal he couldn't name. A few hard-cooked eggs, another crock of butter, another bottle of brandy. And down at the bottom, this time, was a cold smoked bird of some kind—not chicken, but duck or pheasant. He stared at it in delight. It had to be for supper, as it wouldn't keep any longer than overnight. His fingers itched to tear it apart, but his conscience berated him. Yet he had not been told not to eat it. He wavered shortly before temptation, then ripped off a wing and devoured it.

He leaned against the wall and licked his fingers thoroughly, sighing aloud several times. The taste of meat—the slow-roasted juiciness and crisp skin—was a long-forgotten pleasure. He covered the rest of the bird, content now to wait for his sister and her husband. The thought of their current whereabouts—at the church for his brother's funeral service—made him sigh.

Slowly, he packed the food away, then looked through the parcels for his new clothes. He found two new nightshirts, both identical, and a nightgown that was obviously for Molly. He found slippers for himself and for her, and a short navy blue coat that looked as if it had been made for a sailor. There was another shawl—this one green—and several items of underclothes. He was tempted to strip and don a new nightshirt, then thought he might ask for a bath when they returned. That way he'd be clean from the skin out.

He should be, he knew, completely content. But a restlessness grew in him as it had earlier in the day. He fidgeted for a few minutes, then stopped to think. What was wrong with him? He had everything he needed for the moment. Then it struck him that he was bored.

He'd not been bored for a long, long time. For much of a year he had been too busy taking care of his mother and brother to even stop and think about anything but the immediate present. After his mother's death, he'd been too scared and then too sick to care about anything at all. Now, he had food and shelter and a real chance to recover, and he wanted to know what the future would bring. He wanted to get up and go to Wexford and see the sights and the sounds of the city. He wanted to meet new people—people who would not remind him of the sorrow and death he had seen in this place. He wanted to start living again. And maybe he, too, would meet someone and marry. He wondered how old the nieces were.

"Look at ye! One little day ago ye didn't give a damn about livin' or dyin', and wishin' tomorrow would never even come because it was bound to be worse than today. One little day ago..."

He edged over to the side of the bed, dangled his legs and slid slowly off. His feet touched the ground but his knees buckled beneath him. He flipped himself over, grabbing at the covers, managing to pull himself back onto the bed just before he fell.

"Whew! That was close! Perhaps tomorrow..."

A shout came from outside his window, and he crept up to the head of the bed and looked out. The publican was there with the kitchen lad in his grasp, and he was shouting and slapping the boy about the head and ears while the boy tried to shake his arm free and protect himself all at once.

"Whew!" said Johnny again, his good fortune striking him sharply. "At least I'm not that poor lad!"

Chapter 6

THE MASS HAD BEEN SAID and the coffin carried to the gravesite. The wind had died down and clouds gathered overhead, as if in compact with the mourners. Molly was weeping softly and John Patrick stood with his shoulder just touching hers. Aside from the priest, the only other person present was the blacksmith, who had dug the grave and both built and helped to carry the coffin. He was a huge young man who resembled nothing less than the trunk of a tree, and who confessed to no other name than "Tiny". He was prematurely bald and the black fringe of his hair was in dire need of a trim.

He'd been helpful to John Patrick in many ways. They'd met when the Easterner needed to put up his donkeys and cart, and they had taken an instant liking to one another. It was Tiny who had directed him to Clare for the clothes he wanted, and lent him a horse to make the journey shorter. And today, the smith had begun adding a shelter to the cart to make it a viable all-weather transport for the sick boy.

Although he did not own the livery, Tiny had charge of the Earl's horses. The Earl and his wife had a penchant for hunting in large parties and owned several dozen animals. The smith had been responsible not only for their shoes but for their overall health, and had been paid a handsome wage for his talents. Before the blight, he had been one of the most wealthy and respected of the native villagers. Since then, his funds had been sorely depleted: he'd offered Father Boylan half of his savings the first year of the famine. From previous experience, both men had known that the village would be hard hit, but had assumed the next year's crop would be good. As it was not to be, Tiny offered half of what he had left the second year, and even half of the remainder in the past summer when it became apparent that the crop was bad for this third year in a row. He had enough now for his own needs, but if the famine were to persist, by another spring there'd be nothing at all left. He considered it quite likely, however, should that come to pass, neither would there be any left in the village to care for.

He prayed aloud with the others, his mind filled with thoughts of the villagers who had passed before, most notably his lovely young wife. She had died in childbirth four years earlier. The child had died too, and he mourned them every day. Glancing up, he caught sight of the kitchen lad from the pub by the gate to the cemetery, gesticulating wildly and jumping up and down on one foot. Quietly, unobtrusively, he walked to the boy and bent to hear his whispered words, then returned to catch John Patrick by the sleeve and murmur in his ear.

The Easterner looked up, startled, and saw the boy still waving his arms about. The service was almost over. Tiny bent to pick up a handful of dirt and throw it in on the coffin. The priest glanced at him as Tiny made a "hurry-up" sign. With a frown, Father Boylan gave the final blessing and heard Molly's soft, "Amen."

Tiny followed as John Patrick took his bride by the arm and drew her away. She began to protest as the boy ran up to them.

"H-hurry, sir. Ye must hurry!"

"Will you come?" John Patrick asked of Tiny, who gave him a nod in response. "You stay here, lad. Stay right here, d'ye understand?"

Father Boylan laid a hand on the lad's shoulder. "He'll stay. He'll be here until you come back."

John Patrick set off at full stride, anger consuming him. Tiny matched him step for step as Molly ran behind.

"Oh, what's happening? What's wrong?" But they did not answer.

At the door to the public house, Johnny lay outside on the ground, their belongings heaped in piles around him. His face was dirty and streaked with tears. Molly ran to kneel beside him.

"What's happened? Oh, are you hurt?" He had no time to answer before John Patrick barked an order to Tiny.

"Bring him." The smith scooped the boy into his arms, followed the Easterner into the tavern.

The publican stood at the bar with an old musket at the ready, but before he could so much as aim it, John Patrick snatched it away and threw it into the corner. He grabbed the fat man by the collar and his whole body seemed to grow bigger—his broad shoulders stretched his coat and his arms bulged. His face livid, he slapped the publican across the top of his head.

"Show me to your room," Tiny said to Molly. She turned to him and then back to her husband. He was shouting now at the fat man and slapping his face, accusing him of all manner of evil. "Show me your room," the smith ordered.

The shouting followed them up the stairs.

"You fat, greasy pig of a man! You sodden, overblown excuse for a human!" Again the sound of a slap. "Have you no honor? No compassion for the sick?" A spluttered response, and another slap. "If you touch that boy again, I'll kill you!"

Molly gasped as Tiny deposited her brother on the bed. The smith left, closing them in behind him. She stared at the door. She could hear her husband still shouting but could not distinguish the words. She was inordinately proud and frightened at the same time. If the constabulary should come today...

"Sissie..." Johnny called weakly. She saw his tears and the shaking of his shoulders, and ran to hug him.

"Oh, Johnny darlin', what's happened? Did he hurt you?"

"No." He breathed it into her shoulder, clinging and shuddering. "He came and hauled me out..."

She pushed him gently back, wiped his tears away with her apron. "Did you not latch the door?"

Her brother nodded vigorously and pointed. It was plain to see that the door had been forced. She went to inspect it, heard more shouting and peeked out.

Her husband's voice roared up the stairs. "Ye bastard spawn of a lop-eared fornicating sow..."

"Oh, my Lord!" Swiftly, she crossed herself then turned and shut the door, her ears burning. Such profanity she had seldom heard in her life, and certainly not at that volume. Her Da and O'Fagan had both cursed in her presence, but muttered their words. Ashamed as she was for hearing this, pride swelled in her breast. She raised her hands to her burning cheeks, scarcely daring to look at her brother, but a lop-sided grin had taken the place of tears.

"Johnny, don't you ever say words like that!"

"Not me, Sissie. I couldn't ever—" He broke into giggles. "I couldn't ever do it so good!"

"Hush, you wicked boy!" She ran back to him, slapped at his hand but he pulled it too quickly away. He giggled again and she had to fight to keep a smile from her face. She strained her ears but the shouting had stopped.

Johnny leaned against the wall, took Molly's hand and held it tightly. "He's a rare 'un, ain't he, Sis?"

She stopped fighting the smile. "Aye, that he is." She looked out the window, saw him with Tiny. The blacksmith's hand was firmly on his arm but her husband was not resisting. They strode boldly across the square, heading to the church or the livery. "Aye, that he is," she repeated, watching until they were out of sight. She stood up and smoothed her apron absently. "Perhaps I should go down and gather up our things."

"No. No, I don't think he would be pleased. You don't know what that 'spawn of a lop-eared sow' might do. Best not to give him the chance to harm ye."

She regarded him seriously. "All right. But I am hungry. It's the first I've had communion in a long while. I'd forgotten how hungry I get after."

"What was it like, Molly? The service, I mean."

"Ah, Johnny, it was grand." Her voice took on a beautiful, peaceful tone. "It was the High Mass, in Latin and with the singing, too. I'd forgotten parts of it, but *he* knew it all. And when we prayed for the dead, the father asked blessings for Willie, and for Mam and Da.

"William Daniel O'Brien, the Father said. And then Margaret Mary O'Brien and Francis James O'Brien. Just like that—their whole names said right out loud. And then we prayed for the sick—for Bridie O'Fagan and Martin Kiernan." Her eyes gleamed as she added, "And for John Francis O'Brien!"

"Did ye really?" Her brother leaned toward her. "Did the Father say my name right out loud in church?"

"Aye."

"D'ye think the Lord heard it?"

"Of course! How can you ask such a thing?"

He lay back again, his mouth slightly open. They sat in silence for some minutes.

"Johnny, do you remember when the constables were last here?" Molly asked in a deliberately casual voice.

"Saturday week. Remember, O'Fagan came and told us they'd been up to see to the Earl's property."

"Aye." Her breath came out in a sigh. They would not be back then for two weeks or more. There'd been a time when the English dragoons would spend a week out of every fortnight in the village. But there'd been no trouble here for more than a year—or at least no trouble they'd thought worth their attention. Now they would still show up every month, but stay only as long as they needed to patrol the countryside.

But what if that fat pig sent for them? Would he know where to find them? And who would he send anyway? The kitchen lad? But he was at the church, and the Father said he was to stay there. Tiny wouldn't go, nor any of the villagers. The Earl was gone and every one of his servants gone with him, leaving only his overseer behind. The publican's fat, useless wife never went anywhere—said it made her sick to travel. They'd be traveling soon themselves. How long would it take? She occupied her mind with the thought of the trip that lay before them and forgot her fears and her hunger. For once, at least, she knew it was temporary—they would eat again as soon as her husband returned.

IT WAS TINY WHO CAME back first, with an armload of their possessions and a pocketful of staples to mend the latch. Molly snatched at the pile of things he tossed on the bed, sought and found a small wooden doll with jointed arms and legs. The paint on her sweet face had faded, but Molly set her lovingly on the bureau and smoothed her tattered dress. The doll had been a gift from her Da. Stroking the dress, Molly peered out the window, willing her husband to come quickly.

Tiny was scratching his bald pate—the framework had been shattered when the lock was forced. "Need more tools," he said. "Back in a minute."

He was as good as his word, and brought the rest of their belongings up with him.

"Bit of a mess," he said in way of apology.

"It's fine," Molly replied. Fortunately, most of the food was still wrapped, though there was a coating of dust on everything and the ragged clothing she had doffed earlier in the day was bunched in with the rest. She sorted them out and dumped them in the corner without regret. She put the food on the chest and began to open the remaining parcels.

"Here's your nightshirt, Johnny. And what's this?" She held up a nightdress. "Oh, my..."

"Pretty, ain't it?"

"Oh, my!" There was no doubt it was for her. She stroked the white cotton hesitantly—it was the most beautiful thing she'd ever owned, with a lace collar, light green smocking, and pale yellow flowers embroidered on the yoke. It was soft and crisp at the same time, and she hugged it against her as if fearing it would disappear.

"Nice," said Tiny.

"And almost long enough," Johnny chimed in with that devilish grin.

"Oh, you!" Molly stuck her tongue out at him. Reluctantly she folded the gown and put it in the bureau. But she continued her chore of sorting and folding with a soft glow on her face. And the smile of delight she gave to John Patrick when he returned was enough to stop his heart in its tracks.

Chapter 7

EVENING WAS UPON THEM again. All that remained of the pheasant was a pile of bones, Johnny having gnawed every scrap of meat from them. It was with difficulty that John Patrick convinced him to save the rest of the bread and honey for breakfast.

"My belly is stretched to its limit," Johnny admitted grudgingly, "but my mouth wants that sweet taste again." John Patrick opened the jar and let him stick his finger in it one last time.

Now the boy leaned into the corner propped up by pillows, as his sister yawned mightily. John Patrick put his pipe on the bureau, stood and stretched, his hands reaching the beams of the ceiling. He smiled down at his bride.

"Think I'll walk for a bit," he told her, retrieving his coat from the bedpost and shrugging into it. He checked in the pocket for the piece of charcoal he'd taken from Tiny's forge earlier.

"I'll come with you," she offered.

"Nay, love. You stay here and see that our boy does not explode." He ruffled the lad's dark hair. "I've not seen such gluttony since Judas was a pup!"

Molly laughed up at him, then turned serious. "I want to bring the hammer to O'Fagan."

"Time enough for that tomorrow. We'll not be leaving until Tiny finishes with the cart—at least a day more, he tells me."

"Of course." Molly sank back against the bed. He was glad she was so amenable. He could see that she was on the verge of exhaustion—her eyelids drooping every few seconds and her hands listless in her lap. He dropped a kiss on her forehead.

"I'll not be long. Perhaps I'll stop and see the Father for a few minutes. You should get some rest. And you, too, boy-o."

Johnny belched in response and his sister looked daggers at him.

"S'cuse me," he chirped. "Help me on with that new nightshirt, Sissie."

As she complied, John Patrick turned quickly and left them. Molly settled her brother in under the blankets, then bade him close his eyes while she changed into her own nightclothes.

"Lovely," he told her when she allowed him to look. "Ye look like an angel in the Book of Saints."

His sister blushed furiously. "Silly boy," she murmured. But in truth she felt like an angel—or perhaps like the Earl's daughter. She pulled back the blankets on her bed and climbed in with a grateful prayer.

They talked for a while about their journey, wondering aloud what they would find at the other end. But when her voice grew weaker, Johnny ceased his rambling and watched her fall into a deep sleep.

He wasn't tired enough to sleep, so stared out the window. He was surprised to see John Patrick coming, not from the smithy or the church, but from the lane that led to their croft. And to the Earl's lands. He was even more surprised to notice that Molly's hammer was in his brother-in-law's hand. But when John Patrick entered the room a few moments later, he signaled for silence. The boy watched while he put the hammer in its corner and took off his coat and vest. Then he turned to look out the window again to provide the older man with some privacy.

"Good night, lad," he heard the Easterner say. He looked around, held back the question on his lips, and murmured a response. Molly was sleeping on the edge of the bed, one arm dangling. John Patrick slipped in behind her and covered himself with an extra blanket. Then

Johnny crept down beneath his own covers, frowning slightly, and went promptly to sleep.

IT WAS FIRST LIGHT and a single bird was singing when Molly awoke. A crisp breeze was making its way through the open window and her face was cold. She'd gotten used to being cold and at first, she did not understand why the rest of her was so warm. She raised her head, saw the blankets that covered her and then the sleeve of her nightdress. She felt the weight of John Patrick's arm around her waist. A long sigh passed her lips. She slid backwards a little so she was resting against his chest. He was there—he was real and strong and warm. It seemed impossible. She would never break another rock to feed her brothers. *My brother,* she corrected herself, *for there's only me and Johnny left now. My Willie's gone.* She tried to smother a sob in her pillow.

"Hush, *mavourneen.*" The words were infinitely tender and he was stroking her hair, as her Da used to do. She turned to him, buried her face in his chest, and she cried for all of them—her Da, her Mam and Willie, for the children she had played with and their parents and grandparents, for the babies that had been born dead and those that had died so shortly after birth. For the people who had been kind to her and had suffered losses as great as her own. And for herself and Johnny, being the sole remains of their family. And finally, for the sheer relief of passing the responsibility for their two lives into another's hands.

John Patrick held her tight and tried to soothe her. Her body was shaking but her grief was silent, punctuated only by an occasional gulping sob. He understood—she'd never had a real chance to grieve for her family before. Yet he worried that her strength would not be enough to see the storm through. It was only gradually that her tears subsided.

"Hush, my love," he whispered. He looked down into the eyes of exhaustion. He kissed her hair and her white brow and she turned her face against him once more. He held her tightly, tenderly, as her body slowly stopped shaking and the hands that had clutched at his nightshirt loosened their grip. He wrapped the blankets closely around her and bent his head over hers.

"Go to sleep, *mavourneen*," he murmured. "'Twill all be right now."

She searched his face for a long moment, then dropped her head again to his shoulder. Within minutes she was asleep.

Thank you, Lord, for this girl—this woman. Thank you for this chance to make some small part of a great wrong, right. Thank you for this love I feel—this need for her. Let me be her strength, for she has so little left. Let me always protect her, and love her as I do at this moment. And someday, let her love me, too.

HE SLEPT TOO FOR A little while, but he had business to complete before they could leave for Wexford and it was already Saturday. He got up quietly, pleased to notice that Molly simply rolled to the edge of the bed, still soundly asleep. He watched as she let one arm dangle out from under the covers and over the side. *She must sleep that way always.* He realized he'd been watching her for several minutes and bestirred himself to action.

He gathered up a few items from the room, including a heavy canvas satchel. Then he locked himself in the next room. He had, after all, paid for it for three days and so far used it only one. He removed a few pieces of clothing and a false bottom from the bag and drew out several stacks of paper money and a few small bags of coins.

This was the money with which he was to have purchased the oats. He counted it first and then he divided it into fifteen equal piles.

The trip from Wexford had taken him ten days—he would allow four extra days for their return journey, for he did not think that

Johnny was strong enough to ride in the cart for ten hours a day, even lying in a bed of straw. The fifteenth pile he would save for emergencies.

He sat smoking his pipe for a long time after he completed his chore. The money came to much more than he needed for food and shelter, and he had enough in his pocket to pay for Tiny's services and outfit their cart properly, including victuals for the ever-hungry boy. They would buy whatever food was available on the way.

It was not, strictly speaking, his money. It belonged to the business. He had almost enough in savings to repay it if need be, and knew that his grandfather would consider the balance a loan and give him whatever time it took to pay it back. Or his mother might lend it to him if the business needed it right away. He thought of subtracting an equal amount from each pile and using only half of what he had, but after much consideration, he left things as they were.

He wrapped each bundle individually in handkerchiefs and strips torn from Johnny's old nightshirt. He would then have only to remove a single bundle each day. He put them in the bag and refitted the bottom, then took it to his own room, where he found Johnny almost hanging out the window.

"Where's your sister?" he asked.

"She took the chamber pot out back—come and see this."

John Patrick joined him and saw the priest in agitated conversation with the Protestant pastor and another man.

"I can't hear them," Johnny complained. "That's the Earl's steward and he was shoutin' about somethin'—I think he said oats or goats. Why don't ye go see?"

"What business is it of mine?"

The boy frowned at him. "Must it be yer business? Haven't ye any plain curiosity?"

"About what?" Molly asked from the doorway. She came to join them at the window. "Oh, that..."

"What is it?" her brother demanded. "What's going on?"

"Well, the Earl's man came to complain to the pastor. He said someone opened the granary doors last night and the farmers are taking the oats—just carting them away."

"They're not stealing it?" Johnny was aghast. The Irish tenant farmer might beg or cajole, use trickery or even act the fool to get what he needed, but for six hundred years the punishment for theft had been both swift and merciless, and in this part of the country at least, it was unheard of.

"The father and the pastor both said it's not stealing," Molly answered thoughtfully. "There's writing on the door itself that says the grain is free, so those that are taking it are not to blame. But someone broke the lock and the Earl's man can't shut the doors. Tiny won't help him fix it, because they can't say if he'll be paid. They say only the man who did it would be responsible."

"D'they know who it is?"

"Nay." Molly turned to make up the bed, but Johnny stared at John Patrick. The older man lit his pipe with an air of nonchalance, then reached out to ruffle the boy's black hair.

"I wouldn't worry about it, lad," he said, a faint glimmer in his eye. "I'm sure it's not a deed will be laid to anyone's door."

"But the dragoons..."

"Aren't due for another two weeks, and the evidence will have been eaten by then, I'll vow. Don't worry, lad." He dropped his voice so that Molly would not hear. "By the time the investigation starts, no one will remember we've been here. And Tiny, I believe, will mention a vagrant coming through, so no one else will be held to blame."

"Are ye sure?" the boy whispered.

"Positively. Put it out of your mind. None will be harmed, and many are aided."

Johnny settled back, his eyes fixed thoughtfully on John Patrick's. What he saw there was certainty, so he allowed himself to accept it. The older man reached for his head again.

"If ye're sure," he acquiesced.

"I am."

The ruffling of his hair was a bit more vigorous than previously and Johnny smiled proudly—he'd been entrusted with a secret, one that would mean a man's freedom, if not his life. In that moment he felt he'd become a man, and he would trust as he had been trusted.

"As ye say," he responded. "But where, pray tell, would my breakfast be?

Chapter 8

IN THE LATE AFTERNOON, John Patrick and Molly walked to O'Fagan's croft, where tearful goodbyes were outweighed only by tearful gratitude, as she offered him her sledgehammer and John Patrick pressed a handful of coins into his palm.

"For the children," the Easterner said, when O'Fagan attempted to refuse.

"Take it!" his wife hissed in his ear. "Take it an' damn yer pride!" To John Patrick she turned a face of humility and gratitude. "Thank 'ee, sir. An' God bless 'ee."

"'Tis I that owe you thanks," he replied. "Molly has told me of your care for her and her brothers. I cannot thank you enough."

"We's neighbors, sir. We done what we could."

"Aye," he said, for the doctrine was familiar. His mother and his uncles had drilled it into him from birth. "As I will do for you if ever I can."

She nodded thoughtfully and watched her husband stuff the coins deeply into his waistcoat pocket. O'Fagan was a little man and had obviously once been quite stout. Below the corded muscles of his upper arms hung empty flaps of skin. He grinned at John Patrick, showing wide gaps in his teeth.

"Yon Molly is a fine girl, an' mebbe one day we'll come t' see ye in Wexford. Wherever that may be."

"You'll be most welcome." John Patrick wrung the offered hand. "The Father can direct you if you wish." But O'Fagan had turned to Molly, whose cheeks were streaked with tears. He shooed the children

47

away from her skirts and his wife relieved her of the baby in her arms. He held her hands tightly.

"Ye be a good girl," he said sternly, but with a smile of pure devotion.

"Oh, I will. And do come to see us. Please."

"If the Lord is willin'," he promised in turn. "Now go say yer good-bye to Grainne."

A tiny, wizened, white-haired woman had been waiting by the cottage door. She stepped forward and John Patrick saw with amazement that she hardly reached to Molly's waist.

"Sit down, child," she commanded, drawing the girl to a crude bench. She took Molly's face between her hands. "Naught to cry fer," she gently admonished. "'Tis a good thing that's happened."

"I know. But I will miss you all so much."

"For a while." The old lady's brown, wrinkled face came close to Molly's. " 'Twill be hard yet awhile. But if ye are strong, an' if ye have faith, there will be the very great happiness in yer life.

"Be strong. Have faith. An' there will be great happiness." Molly nodded and the old woman kissed her on both cheeks. "God bless ye, child. An' send ye health."

"Thank you," Molly whispered. "God bless you, too."

There were more tears and more blessings before they walked back to the inn in the dusk. John Patrick was quiet, wondering what more he could do to help these poor people with their ingrained philosophy of neighborliness. Wondering how his country had devolved to this state of affairs when both of its classes—society and worker—both of them held this philosophy so dearly that it became one of life's first lessons for all of her children. *Things must change. But how can I change them?*

He stopped for a moment to refill his pipe, and when he turned to Molly, her hands were twisted in her apron. He took a step back and sat on the stump of an oak tree, removed his pipe from his mouth and spoke gently to her.

"What is it, *colleen*?" He waited while she found her courage, his patience more an ingrained trait than mere habit.

"I... I..." She looked at him, then down at her feet and away into the trees. Her words tumbled out. "I cannot believe all that's happened. I feel I'm dreaming and about to wake up. I don't know how to say... what I want... what I need to say... there are not any words. 'Thank you' is in my mind, but it seems not enough.

"No, please, let me finish. I know Johnny would be dying if it weren't for you. I think I might be dying, too. I didn't know how to go on any longer—I didn't know how I would feed him, even after Willie was gone. I knew there was no hope for him—I was so afraid there was no hope for us. We needed you... I needed you..."

She looked up at him finally, her breath catching in her throat. But when he opened his mouth to speak, she waved him off. "Please..."

He settled in and waited, drawing on his now-empty pipe.

Her words, when they came, were less jumbled, more hesitant. "You knew what I meant to do. You could have let me. I don't know why you didn't... but I am so grateful. I don't have words to tell you. You have given us so much—you have saved us. And yet you are not asking for what is yours by right. I want to... I need to... do you not find me...?"

"Enough." His voice was gentle, even tender, though the word was harsh. Molly fell silent. He put his pipe away and held his hand out to her. She came close and clutched at it, and he stood and drew her towards him.

"You are the most beautiful creature on God's earth," he told her. Her head fell to his shoulder and he held her for a minute, then stood her up to face him before he spoke. "When I first saw you by the river, I thought you meant to do away with yourself. Now, hush—you've had your say and it's now mine.

"I fell in love with you, Molly, in that single instant. I could not let you destroy yourself. So I stopped you. I had to. And... suddenly it seemed to me that the responsibility for your life was mine. Later, when I learned what you truly meant to do, I could not abdicate that responsibility. What kind of a man would I be if I let you do that?" He chucked her gently under the chin. "What kind of man would I be?"

Molly shook her head but did not answer.

"l could not let you do that," he said, "and yet I knew you would not accept my help if you could not somehow pay me. So I let you think it for long enough to make a plan. And the plan was to marry you. It would keep us both from sin, and give me the right to help you.

"I love you, Molly *bawn*." He reached out and stroked her cheek with one finger, the first purely sensual movement he had made. "But I know that you do not love me. It is too soon, and it may never be." She started to protest, but the words died on her lips. "I do not want your body, Molly. Not without your heart. I do not want you to feel obligated to love me."

"But then... what do you want of me?"

"I want you to rest and get strong. You've barely the strength of a bird just now. I want you to care for Johnny. I believe we can make him well. And I want you to be with me, so that I can protect you and take care of you. And someday, God willing, you will love me, too.

"And then, only then, will we live as husband and wife." He gathered her into his arms once more, buried his hand deep in her bright, unruly hair and pressed his lips against hers for a brief and tender kiss.

"I love you, Molly *bawn*," he whispered. "And I will love you for all of my life. I promise."

Chapter 9

THE RIVER RAN THROUGH the village about a quarter mile from the inn. Molly dawdled along in the morning sun, a bucket swinging from her hand. They were due to leave for Wexford within the hour. She knew that John Patrick had left many gifts behind for her friend O'Fagan, for Tiny, and for the Father and his church. It seemed that everyone had benefited. But still she was not sure she wanted to go. She was frightened and she was eager. Above all else, she was sad.

Her brother had no such problem. She could just picture him—so eager to go, so excited to hear about the sea and the fishing boats and the seabirds on the wing. He made John Patrick talk for hours about the gulls with their crying and laughing and scavenging for every scrap of fish or fin left on the docks. He begged for tales of the fishermen and the smell of the fish and the brine, of the hardships at sea and the taste of fresh salmon baked in a potato crust—crunchy and light, salty and sweet all at once. And again of the seabirds and their noise, and the way they flew inland to warn of coming rain.

She came to the water and squatted down to fill her bucket, then placed it on the ground and leaned back a little on her heels, wrapping her arms around her legs. She stared into the water, let the little rippling waves touch her toes and the hem of her dress. The sun beat lusciously upon her shoulders and the light morning wind played with the unruly tendrils that had escaped her braid. He said there was always a breeze by the seaside, except when the tide turned and it died down to change direction with the flow of the water. He said his family would welcome them with open arms. He said there was a flat above the store they owned, where they all lived together, and a pier not more than three shops away. He said there was food and medicine and everything she would ever need.

She gazed at her reflection in the water, then jumped up to grab her bucket and stride swiftly back to the inn. Her mind was made up. She would leave the past in this tiny village and look for the future by the seaside.

By midday the cart was ready. Johnny was so stirred up about the journey, he'd almost made himself sick. He'd been thrilled to hear that his name had again been mentioned at Sunday's Mass, and most of the neighbors had come to wish him and his sister Godspeed. Too many jugs of porter had been opened, and her brother's head had been reeling when Molly declared a moratorium on both visitors and liquor.

Tiny had outfitted the cart with a thick bed of straw overlaid with canvas, so that the boy might lay comfortably. Another canvas was stretched on iron crosspieces that ran from the front seat to the rear of the cart. It could be folded over to let in the sun, or drawn completely to keep out both sun and rain.

"'Tis better than many a bed I've had," the boy joked as John Patrick settled him in.

"And better than some you're likely to have in the future!" the older man retorted with a grin. Not for the first time, he wondered about the effect those bright eyes would have on his nieces.

The days of their journey fell into a pattern. The early autumn weather stayed unseasonably warm as they went from one tiny village to the next, avoiding the larger towns. Each day's travel depended upon the strength of the boy. They rested often, taking lengthy breaks in the midafternoon, sheltering in shady glades from the glare of the sun or from sudden, short storms. They stopped each evening at a public house if there was one, but on several occasions slept in and under the cart. Once they slept in an ancient cemetery, for the village John Patrick had been told of was no longer standing—all the cottages and shepherds' huts razed by the landlord to make pasture for his horses. Only the shell of the church remained.

Molly would wake each morning with the birds and get herself ready, knowing that they would not leave until her brother wakened on his own. She would walk around the neighboring woods or along a stream for miles, stretching her legs in preparation for the day's ride. Forced inactivity was making her nervous—her body was used to hard labor and her muscles seemed to protest too much rest. Sometimes she would walk beside the cart all afternoon, her swinging stride keeping the tempo of the donkeys' measured tread.

Their second cart held preserved food they had brought wherever possible, and the donkey who pulled it needed little direction, following his brothers and the first cart willingly. John Patrick paid generously for any food available, knowing that the money was of more use to the paupers. And every morning he marked on a hand-drawn map the names and locations of the villages they visited, the population and the name of at least one citizen, usually the priest or deacon resident. If there were no clergymen, he would ask among the villagers, posing innocuous questions about the town's history and circumstances. From the resulting gossip, he would determine the man held in highest esteem and later, out of their sight, he would write down that name on his list.

One morning, Molly returned from her streamside ablutions to observe her husband in argument with the Protestant clergyman. John Patrick's usual calm assurance was certainly gone, his hands waving as his voice barked. She stopped in her tracks, amazed at his words.

"... as bad as the devil himself! ... no right... blame these poor innocents... are ye daft?"

The minister's reply was lost in the breeze, but there was anger in his demeanor.

"Pah!" John Patrick flung his pipe to the ground and pushed his face up into the preacher's. "Ye're the devil's own spawn! Hell's too good a place for the likes of ye!"

The preacher stood silent, his mouth hanging open, as his antagonist turned on his heel and strode away.

Molly ran to her husband's side and caught at his sleeve. "What's wrong?" she cried. "Oh, why did you...?" His words had shocked her, but no more than the rough shake he gave his arm to release her grip.

"Leave be," he growled. His hand searched blindly though his pockets for his pipe. "Damn!"

"You've no right to speak to me like that!"

It was a moment before the words got through to him. He turned to her, saw her head held high and proud, though her chin was trembling and tears imminent. The morning sun cast bright golden lights among the strands of her flaming hair. His heart leaped in his breast and he hung his head.

"You've..." Her voice faltered.

"No, my dear," he answered, meeting her proud eyes. "You're right. And I do apologize.

"Come and sit with me." He had to tug a little at her hand, but she followed him to a crude seat in the square. He knew she was not wholly appeased by his apology. He felt the stiffness in the fingers that usually lay so trustingly in his, and he bore down hard on his emotions.

"I am sorry, Molly *bawn*. I've heard that this morning which makes me so angry I could kill, but I've no right to take it out on you."

"Oh, what is it?" she cried, her fingers closing fast on his. "And what has the preacher to do with it?"

"Everything." He clamped his jaws for a moment, then raised her hand to his lips and pressed it there. He forced himself to make his voice lighter. "That man of God is preaching a sermon every day at the workhouse. They get preaching with their evening meal. As if their lives weren't hard enough!"

"Why is it wrong?"

"What's wrong is that he's telling the dear Catholics that this blight—this famine—is their own fault! That they're paying for their sins with hunger!" He deliberately lowered his voice. "He tells them that if they repent of their evil Papism and become good Anglicans that their souls will be saved, even if their bodies rot!"

"Good Lord!" Molly's hand flew to her lips as if to repudiate the profanity. John Patrick uttered a short, humorless bark of laughter.

"Just so. He calls himself a man of God. And the priest here is just as bad. A fat, greasy pig like your publican. And no charity from him—while his flock is starving, he collects his own tithes and eats like a prince! Men of God..." He shook his head. "What have we come to?" He got out his notebook, pondered over the map and shook his head again. "What have we come to?"

He sighed deeply and folded his map without making a note.

"We'd best be on our way," he said, stuffing the map into a pocket of his waistcoat. He stood and stretched, willing the tension out of his body. He searched absentmindedly, coming up with tobacco pouch and matches but no pipe. He stared at them and sighed.

"I'll get it," Molly offered.

He laughed ruefully. "Seems I'm needing a spare, if I'm not to control my temper."

A small giggle floated back to him as she ran off, and he took himself back to the carts to see if her brother had wakened.

Johnny was still asleep and two bright red spots showed on his cheeks. Frowning, John Patrick put his wrist to the lad's forehead, but found it was not unduly hot. He pulled the canvas over to cover the cart—Johnny liked to watch the stars at night—and found himself saying a prayer for the youth's recovery. He was not so sure as he had told Molly that her brother would survive the trip.

By the time he had the donkeys ready, Molly had fetched fresh water and Johnny was awake. The boy was listless, though, and did not finish his breakfast nor ask about the day's journey ahead. He dropped quickly to sleep and, when they stopped at noon, a pall of sweat had settled over his face and the spots on his cheeks glowed brightly against his pale skin. John Patrick felt his forehead and found it much too hot. He laid the boy on the cool earth under the willows close to the stream they had been following. Molly watched with huge frightened eyes, so he bade her soak some rags in the stream. He stripped off the boy's upper garments and, laying one rag on his forehead, proceeded to wash his chest and arms with another.

Wordlessly Molly followed his example, her hands shaking noticeably as she wrung out the cloths and gently wiped her brother's body. She looked up once, and John Patrick saw her terror. He murmured some encouragement, but it was several silent hours later before the fever broke.

The boy's eyes opened and slowly focused on his sister.

"Sissie..." His voice was weak and cracked. "Wa...ter... plea..."

She ran to the cart for a dipper and filled it in the stream, but she was shaking so violently that she spilled most of the water on herself. John Patrick took the dipper from her, refilled it and returned to find her brother's head resting in Molly's lap, her hands clutching desperately at his. He raised the boy's head and let him sip at the water.

"Not too much," he cautioned, and the bright smile flashed at him. After a few moments, he offered another sip. Putting the dipper aside, he gently closed his hands over Molly's and was shocked at the coldness of them. "*Colleen*, 'tis better now."

Slowly she looked up at him, swallowed hard and nodded. A long shudder passed through her body.

"Sissie," he whispered, releasing one of his hands from her grip and raising it to her cheek. "'Tis all... right... now." His arm dropped weakly but he saw a smile forming on her lips. "That's b-better," he said, exhausted. "I'll just... sleep now."

"Good idea," John Patrick agreed heartily. "Molly *bawn*, fetch some blankets and we'll make a bed under these trees. We'll rest here until tomorrow."

Reluctantly, the girl rose to do his bidding. Her brother was asleep by the time she arranged a bed for him. John Patrick lifted him onto it, then drew Molly away downstream.

"All right, darlin' girl," he whispered, pulling her into his arms. "Let it go now." And he continued to murmur to her as silent sobs racked her body. "All right," he crooned, "all right, my love."

Her strength, he found, was not much greater than her brother's, and when she began to slip from his grasp, he lowered her gently onto the fresh damp grass and pillowed her head on his shoulder as she faded into sleep.

Chapter 10

DEAREST MOTHER,

I hope this letter finds you well. I have much news for you, both of the business and of myself. But first, as to this lad—his name is Timothy, and he caught up to us after a fortnight on the journey, the priest of his village having rescued him from a difficult situation. I've promised him 10 shillings for delivery of this missive; also the prospect of a job on the wharf. He wants to save up for passage to America. It seems there are none of his family left. It's a story I have seen and heard too many times in the past weeks, and I will explain its personal effect on me later in this writing.

As for the business—there will be no oats from the Earl. He has fled the country along with his family and retinue, leaving the grain to rot in the barn in spite of the fact that so many are so desperate for food. What we have read in the newspapers is just the barest account of the reality of this tragedy—I have seen bodies so thin they are little more than bones and yet, somehow, they are still alive. Many are dead along the road, in the ditches, in the villages, and in the cottages, and there is no one with the strength left to bury them. It's fearful I am of an outbreak of plague if something isn't done, yet I am more fearful for those who are still living, for they face the same fate as has met so many of our fellow countrymen.

As for the Earl's grain, I'm pleased to say that some personage unknown has broken the locks of the barn and made it available to the starving of his village. The great damned oaf hadn't even the decency to see their need before he fled, abdicating his responsibility to his dependents.

But enough. I could go on endlessly, so angry am I. But only tell Grandfather and Uncle James that I am using the money they sent to pay the Earl for our trip home and that I will repay them just as soon as I am able.

You are wondering now about "our trip". I am not alone (in more than one sense of the word). For I have taken a wife—a girl I met in the village, a girl of great spirit and courage who was caring for her two young brothers alone, and by breaking rocks to make a road. We have since lost one of the boys, and the other is gravely ill. It is on his behalf that our journey is so slow. Thrice now, we have stopped to let him rest beside a stream or the cool river so that we could make his fever break before it took him. He is weaker than when we started out, in spite of the food I have provided and the great care his sister takes. We travel no more than a few miles each day, in the breezes of morning, and again in the coolth of evening. You must pray for the three of us, that we arrive home together and intact. Then perhaps the doctors will take over his care, or you will find a way to bring him to health. I fear, though, that it may be too late for him, as for so many hundreds of others.

His name is Johnny, by the by, and he is an elegant fellow with a most winning smile. When we get home, we'll have to keep Virginia and Abigail away from him, lest all hell break loose.

And my new bride's name is Mary, tho' she is called Molly by all and sundry. She is a beautiful girl with hair like flames. She is quite tall and—what else can I tell you? Very thin at the moment, but fleshing out day by day since we began the trip. A reasonable amount of food and no work that breaks her back is having a most beneficial affect on her. Worry, though, is taking its toll and our journey will still be a week or more.

There is so much to tell you, but it will have to wait as young Tim is prancing at the bit. Pray for us that we arrive safely. And do your best, please, for Timothy—if there is no place for him at our shop, perhaps Uncle James can find him work at another.

I hope to arrive soonest,
your loving son,
J. P. Donovan

Chapter 11

MOLLY FOUND HERSELF exhausted by inactivity as they sat beneath the willows along the River Nore. For four weeks they had traveled, first following the Shannon and Lough Derg, then east between the Silvermines and Slieve Bloom, south again along the Nore until finally, tomorrow, they would reach the junction of the Nore with the River Barrow and head east to Wexford. Three days more, he had promised, or four. Depending upon how her brother traveled. Three days more, or four.

She was looking forward to a time when she could be barefoot again. Traveling on the road was hard on her legs and feet, and the shoes, though comfortable enough, annoyed her mightily. Button up to put them on, unbutton to take them off. Then button up for the evening's march. A body did not need the kind of slavery shoes imposed.

But Johnny had awaken well today, and she thanked the heavens for their bounty. He was napping now, and the afternoon rest lay before her. The normally cool autumn days had not materialized, and they would not be going on until the shadows were long. Try as she might to hold it in, a little sigh escaped her. It brought a grin from the man at her side and he reached out to ruffle her hair the way he would ruffle her brother's so often.

"Time to fish," he suggested.

"Oh, yes!" she answered breathlessly, pulling at a boot that was only half unbuttoned. With a wrench she managed to remove it, then flung it toward the cart where Johnny slept. Impatiently, she pulled at the other boot. Then, with a louder sigh, she slowed herself down and worked the buttons one by one. Being finally rid of the shoe, she leaped to her feet and grabbed up her skirts, not even waiting for the willow rod John Patrick was holding out to her. At the river's edge, however, she stopped and cautiously made her way down the bank until her toes just touched the water.

This, for Molly, was the best part of their trip—fresh fish was a meal she had loved since childhood. Her Da and O'Fagan would sneak down to the river at dusk and pull in a few fish, aware that if the overseers or dragoons caught them at it they would be flogged or transported. But then her family would join O'Fagan at his remote croft and Grainne would roast the fish with onions, always keeping a pot of cloves simmering to mask the briny smell.

Now there were fewer landlords, overseers and dragoons at large, but it was still prudent to fish outside the villages and off well-traveled paths. Slowly she slipped her feet farther into the water, taking care to move so slowly that the river creatures were not aware of her. One even nibbled at her toes, and she laughed beneath her breath.

John Patrick seated himself on the bank and held out the makeshift pole to her again. This time she took it and the grub he proffered, slipping it expertly onto the bent needle that served as hook. Then with a graceful swing of her arm, she flung the baited hook out as far as it would go and waited silently for a bite.

What a picture she is! With her hair in the breeze and that look of concentration knitted on her brow. And how deft her wrist is, flicking the pole to make the hook dance. I wonder if we could fashion a lure out of a curl of her hair.

She turned to whisper, "Why do you wait?" So he left off his reverie and threw himself into fishing. It wasn't long before they'd caught five fish between them. Hers, of course, were the biggest and the best, a fact that she took full advantage of while cleaning and filleting them.

"Aren't you a handsome one!" she crooned to the largest as her knife deftly opened its belly. She passed it with skin still intact to John Patrick, who had charge of the frying pan. "And you poor little devil, never to grow up to be a big one like your Da over there." With raised eyebrows and shining eyes, she turned to her husband and he had no choice but to laugh.

"She'll get ye," Johnny said, awakening to enjoy this minor clash. "Best fisherman about, is she."

"I've no doubt," her husband rejoined. "Come down here and get your tea." For the boy was able to stand on his own most days, and to walk a bit if he had something to hold onto. Johnny slipped out of the cart and made his way around it, sliding down against the wheel to make a comfortable seat. A plate of fish and bread were passed to him, and a glass of hot tea with honey. When he finished his meal, he demanded anew a story of the seabirds and their flight.

STILL IT WAS FIVE DAYS before they reached Wexford, for Johnny had taken sick the day after they left the cool river paths for the open road. In spite of Molly's prayers for temperate weather, it was too warm. They veered off their chosen path into a wood with a shady little glade and waited two days before his fever broke. With a silent prayer, John Patrick packed their things up again and set off for the coast.

By the time the seabirds could be seen flying overhead, the boy was in a feverish state once more. Molly begged her husband to stop, but he knew it was only hours to home, a doctor, and his mother. So Johnny thrashed and moaned while she tried to hold him still, and the tears ran like a river down her face.

Outside the city proper, John Patrick's young niece was on the lookout and ran to him as soon as she spied him. "Ginnie, thank the Lord! Go fetch the doctor home and tell them we'll be there shortly."

"Yes, Uncle Pat." She stood on her toes to get a peek into the cart.

"Now, girl, now!"

She sprinted off, her blonde braid flying out behind her, and in just moments his cousins appeared, running toward them with a wide flat plank carried between then.

"George!" exclaimed John Patrick. "Thank God!"

"Give the boy here," George commanded. Seeing Molly's distress, he added gently, "'Twill be faster."

She hesitated just a moment, then nodded silently. George and another man pulled Johnny out and laid him on the plank. Then, three by three they quick-stepped away, leaving John Patrick to help his bride down and a younger boy to take the carts and donkeys away.

THE TWO DAYS THAT FOLLOWED were longer than any year Molly remembered. She sat on one side of the large bed in the enormous room every day and stretched herself out on it at night. John Patrick spent many hours with her and Johnny, his quiet ways helping to keep her anxiety at bay. Others came and went—uncles, aunts, cousins, babies—so many she couldn't remember their names. They bought food and drink, clean clothes and bed linens, and stayed for a moment or an hour. They asked what she needed, offered everything they had. When Molly thought about it, she was overwhelmed with gratitude and a very real feeling of kinship—but her mind was mostly consumed with worry, and sometimes grief for her own family. But as she lay next to her brother every night in the darkness, she gave thanks for her new kin before she implored God to spare her Johnny.

Every evening, her mother-in-law came, a small, slender woman with eyes of lightest blue and hands so small they were like a baby's. Katie Donovan sat in a dainty rocking chair and tatted lace. The soft clicking of her bobbins sent Molly to sleep believing they would be safe, so long as Katie sat and made lace.

63

ON THE THIRD MORNING, just before dawn, Johnny woke to a large oaken room. The click of bobbins did, for a moment, make him think he was at home. Then a soft, salty breeze fluttered the lace curtains at the window. *Where am I?* he wondered. In the distance, he heard the laughing cry of a seagull. *Wexford! We've made it at last!* He tried to roll toward the window, but wasn't strong enough. He let out his breath in a low whistle. *Wexford!* A single tear escaped as his eyes fell shut and he slept again.

When next he woke, his sister was sitting beside him on the bed with her head bent and a pink rosary in her hand. He watched her lips move as she told the beads, and added a weak "Amen" when she finished. Her face lit up from within, and a smile spread across her face as tears rolled slowly down her cheeks.

"Hello, Sissie." His voice was barely a whisper. "So we've got here, hey?"

Her nod was quick and violent.

"What have ye there?" The boy reached for the rosary. The pink beads glowed in a way he'd never seen before. He examined them carefully, realizing each bead was slightly different from its fellows, some being not quite round and some with subtle striations weaving through them. "What's it made of?"

Molly had dried her tears on her apron and managed to answer. "It's from a shell—a seashell. Pat's mother gave it to me. They've drilled the beads out of the shell and polished them. Here..." From the dresser against the far wall, she lifted up the biggest shell Johnny could ever have imagined. "Here's the whole shell—I mean another one. It's from the sea, and called a conch shell. The sailors bring them from islands of the Atlantic. Really," she said. "There are dozens of them for sale in the shop across the way. Some are even bigger than this."

"Bigger? If ye say so. Open up them curtains for me, will ye?"

Molly seemed on the verge of argument, but she went instead to do his bidding, pulling aside not only the heavy brocade drapes but the lacy curtains as well. The light, salty breeze entered the room again, and Johnny could almost taste it. He lay still, breathing it in deeply, saying his own prayer of thanks.

After several minutes, Molly asked, "Are you hungry?"

"Thirsty," he answered. She poured water from a crystal carafe into its matching tumbler and passed it to him.

"Gee, they sure live grand here, don't they?" And Molly's words fell over themselves, as she told him of the vast number of other rooms, of mirrors as tall as she and chairs with padded headrests, of a winding long staircase from the shop below. And then on to the cousins, the nieces, her mother-in-law, and the several little children that were also now part of their family.

"She sat all night?" The boy's mouth hung open for a moment. "Just like our Mam when we were mites."

They looked at each other with eyes filling up, then Johnny managed to say, "Perhaps you should tell her—or them, I suppose. And is there perhaps some breakfast?"

"Hah!" The exclamation startled them both, but John Patrick's broad smile had them giggling like babies. The tray he carried made Johnny's face light up. "Mother thought you'd be awake by now. We've some beef broth, plain tea, and a spot of oatmeal."

"Bring it here, man. I'm famished!"

John Patrick obeyed, warning Johnny to eat slowly. Then he went around the bed and sat next to his wife, giving her shoulder a gentle squeeze. He felt the tension in her body slowly dissipate as her brother ate and chattered about the birds wheeling and crying outside his window. It took just a nod or a grunt to satisfy Johnny that they were listening, and when he had finished and fallen back on his pillows, Molly was leaning against her husband's shoulder, his arm around her,

her body totally lax. He dropped a kiss on the top of her head and she looked up with a shy smile.

"Time for you to eat, too." Sensing her refusal, he added, "Virginia will be right up. You need to eat, and then rest." He helped her to her feet and took the tray from Johnny, just as the blonde girl who had met them at the edge of town came in. At the sight of the boy, awake and alert, she dropped a small curtsy and blushed becomingly.

My prayers are answered. I mean, OUR prayers. And she blushed again. Tongue-tied where she was usually garrulous, Ginnie dumped herself into her great-aunt's rocking chair and stared at the boy.

"Just as I thought," John Patrick murmured. Balancing the tray on one hand, he took Molly's hand with the other. "Come, my dear, let's get you taken care of."

Chapter 12

AS SOON AS WORRY FOR the boy's life was alleviated, John Patrick's grandfather called a meeting of the uncles and cousins to discuss the debt. Peter, as patriarch of the family, allowed his grandson to speak first, to clarify the need to have spent the family's money.

"Almost as soon as I left the city, I realized there was infinitely more suffering than we had seen at the docks. West of Wexford County, my travels became a living nightmare. I saw men—thousands of men—and women and children. Walking scarecrows, with their belongings wrapped in little parcels carried in their arms or on their backs. They dragged their parcels and their precious children along, some not even realizing that the children were already dead."

His voice cracked and there was silence for a few moments, until Peter waved his hand, requesting that he continue.

"They begged for rides, and for food—any bite to eat. So at every chance, I bought bread, salt cod, or whatever victuals were available from the sparse stores of the villages.

"I never did see a father take a bite of food. Most were grateful, the mothers making weak curtsies and forcing smiles to their lips. But some were full of scorn, and cursed the benevolence, spitting at my feet, but taking the food as readily as the others had."

He'd learned to hide the food in his wagon and not to disperse it where the petitioners gathered in groups. For on the single occasion he did, the scarecrows fell upon each other, beating one another with sticks and rocks—all to obtain the smallest scrap that was left in the dirt.

"There are soup kitchens in the larger villages, but they can serve only a single meal each day. I passed men and women who had stood in line for hours, their faces lacking all expression. Their children sat on the ground, their bellies big with emptiness, their small faces dirty and streaked with the tears of hunger. Some of them collapsed at my very feet.

"If I'd spent every penny on the way to Clare, I hadn't the wherewithal to feed them. The question beat against my brain—and beats there still. How could this happen in Ireland? How could this happen here?"

Again he halted for several minutes. "These things have lighted such a fire in me—a fire of anger that I fear will never be extinguished. And it was worse, so much worse as we returned. I made this map." He drew it from his waistcoat pocket, handed it to Peter, who passed it automatically to James. "It shows every village we stopped at, every place we camped. And it names the priest or a citizen of consequence—people I believe we can trust to help. For I believe we must help."

Silence greeted his words as he looked from one to another. "We must help," he repeated in a soft voice. "There is no choice, if we are to save our immortal souls."

"Why have we not heard more of this?" James asked. "Where are the news reports?"

"Where would you expect them to be?" Peter demanded. "They have, in fact, been reporting—in the way of omission. When was the last article in the *Times of London* that crowed over the solution to the Irish problem? When before has *The Nation* criticized the Parliament for lack of action on Ireland? Not so much for the peasants' sake—I can see now—but because of the impact on the productivity of the farms and the lesser imports of produce and meat.

"How many deaths have been necessary to affect production in a land of over seven million people? When three-fourths of them, or more, are farm workers?

"Nay, the very absence of reports should have been enough to make us take notice."

Peter then withdrew into silence, appalled by his own ignorance. *When the Society of Friends came to us last month, requesting donations of food and clothing, we gave a fair amount. But only,* he told himself in honesty, *of goods that had not sold and food that was near to spoiling. We asked no questions. We made no real sacrifice. And we charged what we did donate against the tithe.*

And when that ship came in to port from America, fully laden with Indian corn, it had taken three days to find the authority to unload her. There was no bill of lading, no payment due. Even then we did not question.

Are we really that innocent? Or do we just not want to know?

WHILE JAMES AND THE cousins held small whispered conversations, John Patrick walked to one of the long windows that overlooked the quay and watched the whirling of the seabirds. He would pay the business back if necessary, but every penny he could tease or worry into his hands would go to those hapless souls who were victims of his own country's apathy.

Finally, Peter cleared his throat, calling them all back to attention. "That girl of yours—Molly is it? Tell me her story."

And so he did, saying that he had found her at the river and thought she would commit suicide, never mentioning her actual decision. He told of their marriage and of his discussion (as he termed it) with the publican. He did not reiterate his part in breaking open the Earl's storehouse, nor that the boy Timothy he had sent ahead had been the publican's kitchen lad. But he told them how Molly had given

O'Fagan her Da's sledgehammer, the hammer she had been using to break rocks for the road, and the resulting outcry warmed his heart.

"What road?"

It was his Uncle James' voice John Patrick heard above the rest, and James' question that he answered. "A work program for the indigent, Uncle. Molly took her father's place on the road gang. Her only other choice was to leave her brothers alone and go into the workhouse. So she broke rocks and built the road."

"But—" James sputtered.

"A road to where?" demanded his cousin George.

"Nowhere. The road started in the village and went to the river, no farther."

"But..." James began again, and this time they waited for his question. "But how could she do that? She's barely an ounce of flesh on her!"

His nephew shrugged. "That's the work she could get to feed her brothers. She told me also, that if the authorities caught her at it, they'd have stopped her and given her place to a boy."

"But then what...?" Once again, James could not finish his question. He sat back, grimacing and shaking his head.

"Then they'd all have died," Peter stated flatly.

"Yes," John Patrick agreed, and turned back to the window.

It was his Uncle James who came to him, put a hand on his shoulder. "All right, lad. We're agreed. The money has gone for charity. Including what paid for your journey. We'll not ask for reparation. Now as to that map..."

WITH THEIR MINDS FOCUSED on the plight of their countrymen, the family made plans to help. Using the map that John Patrick had made, they sent Timothy and other drivers off with wagonloads of non-perishable foods to the little towns marked upon it, starting with the nearest. The cousins tried to enlist the aid of other local shopkeepers, but all were convinced that the government was taking care of the problem.

"See here." One neighbor pointed at his daily newspaper. "There's not even a mention of the troubles any more."

"Blindness," James stated to the family as they gathered for the evening. "They want to believe their government is handling this. Otherwise their consciences would be bothering them. No one realizes it is the Society of Friends who are doing the work, running a soup kitchen right here in the city for those who have come from inland.

"Our Church of England does nothing. The Catholics are penniless and starving. There's none left but the Quakers to take on this great burden. And not one among our neighbors will so much as donate food to the soup kitchens.

"Lazy, they call them. Shiftless, these men who are but skin and bones, saving up their bread for their children to eat. Ah, darlin'," he said to Molly, seeing the tears that streaked down her cheeks. "I am so sorry." He walked over, took her hand in both of his. "They are great men, these husbands and fathers. And deserve great credit for the sacrifices they make.

"What help we can give, we will give." His family nodded in unison. "And God help those who can give but will not."

Chapter 13

THE DAYS FELL AGAIN into a pattern. John Patrick resumed his duties in the chandler's shop below, covering the luncheon hour for his cousins so that he might later take tea with Molly in her brother's room, for both the doctor and Katie had agreed that their patient was not to get up for several weeks. Molly found herself sleeping late into the mornings. On the one hand she worried that her husband's family would think her lazy, but on the other she could not remember feeling so well. After their noon meal, she stayed with Johnny until tea-time, watching him grow stronger and better every day. The evenings she spent with the family, Virginia and Abigail taking turns sitting with Johnny.

Molly was happy in spite of her lingering grief. At night she lay with her husband's arm around her, and every few days, a new dress or apron or petticoat would appear on her pillow. No one ever took the credit for these gifts, but there was much winking and elbow prodding as she tried to thank them for their generosity. She blossomed under their care, gaining strength and weight, so that after just a few months, none of them save John Patrick remembered the bony, gangling girl that she had been.

Her mother-in-law was well versed in the ancient arts of healing. Some claimed she was a seer, though she would never admit it. But the herbs and broths she recommended for Johnny and for Molly were given credit for their steady recovery. And the tisanes she insisted Molly drink daily were acknowledged as the reason for her returning strength.

But as much as Molly enjoyed them, the days seemed like weeks to Johnny, until he was finally allowed out of bed. For the first few days he was restricted to his room, but when Katie saw that he was able to walk without help, she invited him to join the family for dinner.

"Ah, yes!" exclaimed the boy, making for the door.

"Heh! Should you not first get dressed?"

Johnny looked down at his nightshirt and laughed. "Ye'll excuse me, then, won't ye?" With a bright smile and a birdlike nod of her head, the old lady left the room.

Johnny had seen his sister storing things in the wardrobe from time to time, but was amazed at the number of garments he found within it. He fingered the materials—soft linens, moleskin, fine lawn, beautiful wools and leathers. Breeches and long pants, an overwhelming number of shirts, vests—even one in green velvet. Two waistcoats. And an overcoat.

In the drawers on the side he found silk cravats and numerous undergarments, all of the finest linen, along with leather and suede gloves, woolen stockings, garters, braces, and handkerchiefs. And on the floor of the armoire, three pair of smooth soft leather shoes and a pair of boots. For once in his life, Johnny was struck silent.

He had no knowledge of fashion—indeed he could not remember a time when he had more than two pair of pants, one for work and one for Sunday and both hand-me-downs from Willie. Judiciously, he chose clothing in the same greens, fawn and gold he had seen John Patrick wearing on their trip. He stepped before the long mirror and gave a joyful laugh.

"Look at me!" he told the mirror, patting his chest. "I'm a gentleman now!" Turning sideways and around to admire himself, he laughed again. "Who'd've ever thought..."

Katie was waiting at the top of the stairs. Feeling the need to steady himself, he took her arm, but his renewed strength outmatched the staircase, and the shining smiles that greeted him below made his heart warm through.

The family stood aside to let him and Katie enter. The sight of the great table, filled to capacity, was a shock to him. He felt Katie's reassuring pat on his arm. She led him to a seat next to hers at the foot of the table, and he held her chair as he had seen his Da do for his Mam. A pang of grief stabbed at his heart for days long gone.

Virginia and Abigail jostled for the seat beside him.

"Leave be!" came the command from the head of the table. "Abigail, sit," Peter commanded. Ginnie's bottom lip quivered. "Jim, give your sister your seat and come sit here by me."

Ginnie ran around the table to take the seat opposite Johnny before her great-grandfather could reconsider, and with a strut in his step, Young James seated himself at the right hand of the patriarch.

Conversation, like the food, flowed round the table freely. Johnny listened and ate until he was addressed by Peter.

"So, lad, you're feeling well?"

Johnny nodded vigorously, and tried to swallow the huge piece of bread he had crammed into his mouth.

"Peace be, lad," the old man said. "There will be more food tomorrow." Johnny blushed crimson and managed to choke down the last of his bread.

"Sorry," he mumbled.

"Be not sorry," Peter commanded, "nor ashamed. You have seen too much hardship. Believe me when I tell you, you are of this family now and what is ours is yours."

Johnny nodded, close to tears. The old man continued, "Haven't you any questions to ask of your new family?"

"Well..."

"Out with it, boy."

"How is't your name's O'Connor? I mean... ye're Anglo, ain't ye?"

A slight gasp was heard around the table, and Molly started to shush her brother. But the old man chuckled.

"Aye, lad, we're Anglo for the most part. Who wants to tell the story?"

A chorus of "I will" rang round the table, but it was Young James who was given the honor.

"A long time ago," he began, "my great-great-great-grandmother—is that right, Great-grandfather?"

"One more."

"Ah, my great-great-great... great-grandmother fell in love with a sailor from America. He came to port twice each year and she would wait on the quay to greet him. After awhile, he fell in love with her, too. Being an American, he wasn't all *that* Catholic, so he agreed to convert in order to marry her. And also to give up the sailor's life.

"Her parents were outraged, but the young people didn't care. They married anyway. Now the sailor had lots of money stashed away in America. So he went home to get it and she went with him. They stayed there for several years, and when they came back—with two little children—her parents took them in again.

"The sailor (his name was Liam O'Connor, by the by) decided to open a chandler's shop in Wexford, as all that he knew was ships and the sea. He called his shop 'Wexford Ship Chandlers', and he began to call himself 'Old Wexford', betting that none of any import would remember he had once been Catholic. He passed the store down through the generations. And then it belonged to my great-great-grandfather,"—Young James looked to Peter for approval and got a silent nod—"who was named William O'Connor.

"William was a bold and daring man. He was well over 6 feet tall and strong as an ox, and he never minded what people said. One night he secretly had the sign changed to read 'O'Connor & Sons, Ship Chandlers'. If any noticed, they never mentioned it—at least not to William, for absolute fear of him.

"And eventually everyone got used to the Anglo family with the Catholic name, and the store is still being passed down through the generations. Great-grandfather Peter has retired, and my grandfather James," he said proudly, "is now senior partner."

"And the sign," James interposed, "should now say 'O'Connor *Family* Ship Chandlers.'"

There were quiet murmurs of approval, both for James and Young James. But Johnny was still curious.

"And where does the Donovan come in?" he asked. Silence reigned for a long, long moment.

"That is another story," Katie said quietly, "for another day."

"I'm sorry." The boy was confused and somehow ashamed. "I didn't..."

"Don't fret." Katie patted his arm gently. "We will speak of it another day."

AFTER DINNER EVERY evening the entire family, except for the babies, would gather in a smallish formal room called "Katie's Parlor". The uncles told family stories, and bragging parents recited their children's activities and accomplishments. Airing of disagreements, most of a minor nature, took place, with Katie or James as mediator. Peter sat in a large chair by the fire, seemingly asleep, but his quiet grunts and coughs let the family know when they were off the track.

The evening gatherings quickly became the high point of Molly's day, for the family talked of all that had happened, of the ships that had come in from exotic ports, of the people who had sailed off. And because they helped her put names to everyone in this very large family, and begin to put children with parents. Katie and James were the only children of Peter's who were still living, but there had been four more brothers and each had had a wife and up to six children. Every night before her prayers, Molly recited a litany to herself.

"James's wife is Annabelle and his children are Henry and George. Henry's wife is Charlotte and their children are Young James and Virginia. George's wife is Rosalee and their children are Victoria, Henry, Abigail, Georgie, Albert and—oh, what *is* that baby's name?"

She often gave up in confusion but, gradually, Molly put the families together in order.

The one thing Molly had not expected, and could not get used to, were the shoes. The family wore shoes all day, whether working in the shop or cleaning house—even while sitting and talking. She never saw anyone go barefoot. She had three pair of shoes now, as well as house slippers to wear in the morning and evening. She would run upstairs after supper to put on the slippers as they, at least, were comfortable. But she would often remove them surreptitiously during the evening gatherings, and fold her legs to hide her feet under her skirts. One night Peter noticed and winked at her with a tiny smile on his lips. She blushed crimson, but did not change her habit. It became a game between them—Molly would see how quickly she could hide her shoeless feet, often waiting until Peter was engrossed in conversation with another. She did not often win the challenge, but it was all the more fun for that.

"He's like a great spider," she confided to Johnny one day. Her brother began to protest, but she continued, "A great, kind spider, weaving his web 'round the whole family, making sure everyone is tucked into their proper corner, and no one comes loose."

Johnny studied her for a moment. "For all that he controls everything, he's a most generous man. I like him."

"As do I. I did not once stop to think, while we were on the way, that he could have turned us out. 'Tis a miracle, is it not, that we have not only been taken in, but made part of the family as well?"

"Aye, it is. But it did not surprise me."

"How so?"

"I did not think that your John Patrick could have a family that would do only their duty. He's a rare 'un, Sissie, and the family explains why."

The corners of his sister's mouth twitched as a faint rosy blush rose to her cheeks. "Aye," was all she said, then she kissed him good-night and left the room.

AS HIGHLY AS MOLLY regarded Peter, the old man came close to worshiping her. *She's brought the breath of spring to the family,* he thought as he listened to the younger generations. *No more do they quarrel over trivia; no more are their petty disagreements taken seriously. This girl with her wild hair and shining eyes has taught them what is important—to hold fast to family, and savor the precious moments.*

Some of them, my own Katie included, have broadened out their vowels and lifted the brogue from that girl and her jolly brother. Katie is speaking Gaelic once more, as she did when first she came home, with her babe not even born yet and her husband dead by those bastard dragoons. She and the girl have a bond between them—a bond of pain and suffering and injustice, yet each has joy in her heart.

God help me to find the joy in life again. My grandson John Patrick is so angry—he stops just short of sedition. But in my mind I am already a traitor. To live with this wretched government—this Parliament who will let her people die without a single regret. Bah! If I had the strength and time, I would board the next ship to England and...

But now, a man can only do what he can do. I will give all my stores if need be; I only wish they were enough to feed the whole population.

Chapter 14

AS JOHNNY REGAINED his strength, he began looking for things to do. He preferred the outdoors to sitting with Molly in the library, and he'd walk for hours on the beach, or sit on the dock and watch the gannets, petrels, and gulls drifting overhead. He learned from experience how to predict the weather, and memorized the schedule of the ships that came and went. And still he was bored.

One afternoon after tea, he begged a conference with Katie's brother James, now the senior partner in the family business. Quietly, almost shyly, he requested that he be allowed to help in the shop. James looked him over quite thoroughly. Though he could feel his ears burning, Johnny said nothing more, but presented his most serious face unflinchingly.

"Well, lad," James said at last, "most of what needs doing requires a bit of arithmetic."

Johnny frowned, not sure if he'd been insulted. "I been to school, sir."

"Tell me about it."

"Well, after me chores was done..."

"And what chores were they?"

"I helped me Da with the plantin' and weedin'. Well, me and Willie. Then we milked the goat—that is, when there was a goat to milk."

James nodded. "I see. And then...?"

"Then me and Willie and Molly—she had her own chores, like sweepin' out and washin' up—we went down the fields to the edge of the village and we sat along the hedgerow. 'Twasn't just us—all the neighbor children come together for lessons."

"Who taught you?"

"Why, the priest o' course! We learned our numbers and letters and two-plus-twos. When we was older, we learned the tables... I forget what they were called." James couldn't quite hide a smile with his hand, but Johnny decided against being embarrassed. He could do the work even he could not remember its proper name.

"Multiplication tables?" James asked.

"Aye, that's it. And then some spellin'—Anglo o' course—and sommat about the world and all the countries. And about the government. And catechism."

"You learned catechism? How did the priest manage that?"

"Well, sir..." Johnny hesitated, as it was strictly against the law to teach the Roman Catholic religion, and everyone knew it. But he felt sure that he could trust this man with the secret. "On Tuesday and on Thursday, that's what the priest taught us. We was lined up against the hedgerow, you know, and could sneak in real fast if the dragoons or the Earl's man come 'round." A sly little grin appeared on his lips. "The Earl, he thought the priest was mad. He'd see him walkin' up and down there on the edge of the field, and sometimes wavin' his arms and talkin, talkin', talkin.'" Johnny accompanied his words with the appropriate pantomime and James burst out laughing. After a few seconds, Johnny joined in.

"All right, lad," James said. "We'll give it a go. John Patrick has his hands more than full with the accounts. I'll give him leave to train you on the receipts. If you take to it, fine. If you hate it, we'll see if we can find you something else."

"Thank ye, sir." Johnny took his hand and wrung it hard. "Ye won't be sorry. I'll do my very best for ye."

"Of that I have no doubt." James reached out and, like his nephew John Patrick, ruffled the boy's dark hair.

JOHNNY TOOK TO ACCOUNTING like a duckling to water, and nothing but praise was passed along to Molly. Like her brother, she'd found a way to be useful, and in the kitchen soon gained a reputation of being an excellent hand with left-over meals. She'd initially been shocked to see the amount of food thrown out, but Rosalee and Alice, her new cousins, were happy to learn a way of cooking that kept waste to an absolute minimum.

One evening as the day wound down and the rest of the family was departing Katie's parlor, John Patrick sent his wife to bed with a soft kiss on her cheek.

"I'll be up soon," he promised. He turned back and sat next to his mother, lingering after the cousins were gone.

"*Acushlah*," Katie said, using the Gaelic she preferred for endearments, "what is it that worries you?"

He pulled on his pipe, only to realize it was empty. He placed it on the table in front of them. "Not worried, exactly. But there is something that concerns me."

"And Molly." His mother's voice was soft but sure. She took his left hand in both of hers, then turned it over and traced the love line. "You are married in name only."

Used as he was to her insights, John Patrick was a bit shocked. He stared at her for a moment, then let his eyes drop.

"I promised her..." he began. "It was so quick, so extraordinarily quick. We hadn't even time to learn each other's names. So I promised her..."

"And now it is time."

"I don't know. I've waited for a sign... a kiss... something..."

Katie laughed softly. "Do you believe a girl like Molly knows how to give a sign?" Before John Patrick could reply, she continued, "The sign is not Molly's to give. 'Tis yours."

"But..."

"Nay, not with a kiss, nor with an embrace. Nor yet in the bed. The problem, my boy, is that things have been turned around. By you." She held up a finger to keep him from interrupting. "Oh, I understand there was need then. But there is no longer any need.

"The problem is that Molly became a wife before she ever was courted. The time has come to put things right. It is your place, your responsibility to address this problem, not Molly's."

John Patrick's gaze rose to meet his mother's, and a smile slowly took shape. Katie's eyes twinkled.

"Go forth, my son," she commanded, "and begin to court your wife."

Epilogue

AUTUMN 1850

Molly had taken to wandering down by the wharf in the early autumn evenings after supper. She'd come to love the soft salty air of Wexford, the screams of the wheeling gulls, the left-over smell of fish from the morning's haul. Toward the end of the wharf, a series of barrels, once filled with salt cod, were lashed to the pilings and made a rough bench where the fisherman sat to swap stories in the mornings. But at this time of day, it was deserted—the men and the children gone home to supper and early bed, the women done with their day's duties, save perhaps a bit of darning by the oil lamp.

At this time of day, her twins lay sleeping peacefully. There were plenty to look after them, from the old lady down to 12-year-old Noreen. So many that, in fact, she sometimes had trouble retrieving them for their meals. Molly smiled to herself—the quick, satisfied smile of a cat. Her boys were growing so quickly—twins by the miracle of contiguous birth only. Adam's hair was black as the raven's wing and his eyes were the wildest of blues, while Brian shared her unruly mop of golden red curls and light blue-gray eyes, and had already outstripped his brother in both length and weight. Two small bundles of humanity had sprung from her and, unless she was mistaken, another small bundle formed already.

Molly sat quite still, enjoying the quiet slap of waves against the piers, watching the clouds gather for their daily sally into port. Today they were developing into a fine mist that made her hair even more curly, while the capricious breezes blew wisps of it into her eyes and her mouth. She turned her shoulders so that they rested against the piling and sighed inwardly. She had come to decide what her future would hold.

For her husband, with growing contempt for the ineptitude of the government and its inability to solve or even recognize the problems of its people, had suggested that they emigrate to America.

Her heart quaked at the thought. To leave Ireland! To abandon her home and her brother, the sole surviving member of her family. For Johnny would not go—this she knew without doubt. Her brother loved this seaport, the seabirds, the shop the family owned, and had vowed to make no trip farther than the end of the wharf. And if she weren't mistaken, by Christmas he would be betrothed to Abigail.

She'd be leaving him behind, and did not know if she'd be able. The bond between brother and sister was almost as strong as that between mother and sons, for she had saved him from certain death. A twinge of conscience interrupted her thoughts.

You and Pat saved him. Without Pat, there would have been no saving of anyone.

And it was there, every day for the past week, that her thoughts had stopped and then sailed round and round and round in her head, much as the seabirds circled the seaport.

A wife's place was at her husband's side, yet he had said that it was her decision to make. In one way, it was exciting to think of a sea voyage. Exciting to contemplate a vast new land, to wish for a farm or a wide open space for the children to play and grow. To think of the little village she'd left behind and dream of finding the same in another land.

Her village was gone now—O'Fagan and Tiny had come along in the spring, the only two who had not succumbed to starvation or the hardship of travel. Though the oats had been distributed down to the last kernel, it was too little for too many. Molly had spent hours in the church, praying for the souls of the children and their mothers, their fathers. And for Grainne, O'Fagan's tiny mother-in-law, who had been so very kind to her. And she had cried in the nights, feeling more alone than ever before in her short life.

When those two men had gone off to Canada by way of Liverpool, her husband had broached the subject of America. And was still awaiting her answer.

Molly knew she would have to go. She would have to leave everything precious and dear to her, except for her husband and children, and sail across that staggeringly beautiful sea in one of the enormous ships that were docked at the piers below. She would have to go someplace else—someplace new and unexpected, where she would be the outsider again, where good fortune favored the lucky and the few.

How can I say no?

And it was when she tore her gaze from the sea and turned back to the wharf that she found her mother-in-law sitting beside her.

"What are you doing here?" Molly immediately realized that her question was ungracious. "I mean, you'll catch a chill sitting here! Let us go back."

"In a moment." The old lady stroked the palm of her daughter-in-law's left hand. "How do you feel about the journey?"

"I'm frightened." The admission spilled from Molly's lips before she had a chance to stop it.

"Of course you are. 'Tis a terrifying thing to leave all you know behind. But you have great courage, Molly, and fear will not overtake it."

Molly stared at her, noticing that there was a slight film over the old lady's bright eyes. This was not the first time Katie had read her mind. It somehow comforted her.

"I... think I..."

"You are with child again, and of course we cannot travel until the child is born. We will have many months to make our plans."

"You also... You will come with us?"

"Of course. Molly *bawn*," Katie added seriously, using her son's favorite form of his wife's name. "This change is great, and there are two courses of action open to you. You can suffer it gladly. Or you can suffer it."

Silence passed between the two women, and a kind of peace settled on Molly's spirit. She jumped up and wrapped her cloak around her mother-in-law's shoulders. "Now we must get you home before you catch a chill."

Afterword

DEAR READER,

I hope you enjoyed THE WINDS OF MORNING. If so, I'd appreciate it if you'd share it on your favorite social media site, or recommend it to your local library or book club.

One of the best ways for new readers to find an author is by reading reviews. If you think others might enjoy this novel, then please consider writing a review on your favorite digital retailer or book review site. Just a sentence or two of what you think is all it takes.

Did you like the characters? the plot? Did you find the story believable? inspirational? boring? Are you looking forward to reading new books in the series? Did something in the story impress? dismay? surprise? Your honest opinion would mean the world to me.

Thanks again for your interest in my work.

Giff

What's next for the Donovan family?

WANT TO KNOW WHAT HAPPENS to the Donovans in America? The story picks up about 30 years in the future, with the family settled in the Arizona Territory. Here's an excerpt from Book 1: *Whispers in the Canyon...*

Chapter 1

Spring 1885

The trail split the canyon walls, walls that loomed tall and close and only gradually fell away, clearing the gloom from midday. The rider lifted his hat and drew a sleeve across his brow.

It was much too hot for April. Too quiet. No breeze stirred the aspen leaves. No birds trilled, no squirrels scampered. Even the brook ran silently. His horse's hooves, muffled by dust, sent up gray ghosts that hung in the air for an instant, then drifted back to earth. If he hadn't known better, he'd have assumed this ranch was abandoned.

The walls continued to recede until they were close to a mile apart, and the ribbon of trail wound between meadows newly sprouted and already sere. Willows hid the brook from view here, and the aspens and sycamores grew thickly. But where were the cattle, the horses? Corrals or pens? He'd never seen a more desolate place.

Round the edge of a cottonwood grove, a ramshackle cabin came into view. And there, from the shadow of the sagging porch, the barrel of a rifle pointed straight at his chest.

Pulling the appaloosa up, he lifted his hands to show they held nothing but the reins. A girl stepped out, gripping an old Whitworth rifle. Schooling his features to hide his surprise at her diminutive size, he said nothing, and made no move toward the dark gun that hung low on his left hip.

"Donovan." It was more accusation than query.

"Yes, ma'am."

"What is it you want here?"

His gaze wandered from the dilapidated cabin to the weedy yard, the broken-down fence, the shed that served for a barn—everything bleached to gray by the Arizona sun. Only the new leaves on the trees rescued it from deadly monotony.

"Well?" she challenged, heat rising to her cheeks as his eyes met hers again.

"I've brought some news from town."

"About Russell? I didn't think it was a neighborly visit." Her voice, soft and scented with the bluebells of Texas, bit out the words. "Are you going to say what you have to say? Or just sit on that horse all day?"

Donovan gestured at the rifle. "You won't need that."

"Maybe not, but it stays with me. Tell me what you want."

"Is your father here?"

"Why?"

"How is he?"

She blinked back the tears that jumped to her eyes. "He's never very good anymore."

The rifle drooped. The rider waited, motionless and silent, until she focused on him again.

"May I get down?"

"Do it slowly. Now, take off your gun and hang it on your saddle."

"Yes, ma'am." There was the slightest tone of mockery in his voice as he hung both his gunbelt and hat over the pommel. He cleared his throat, stifling the urge to laugh at the picture she made, holding a rifle almost as long as she was tall. But the morning's events pushed themselves forward in his mind, and when he spoke, his voice was solemn.

"Jesse, we should move away from the house."

"It's that bad?"

He said nothing, but let the slight tilt of his head answer. Jesse turned and walked several yards away from the house, stopping at the broken fence to stare out at a tiny vegetable patch.

As he followed, Adam Donovan was struck by the inconsistencies in her. She was so petite, she could have been taken for a schoolgirl, while to his reckoning she was eighteen or nineteen years old. Her words had been bitter, but her voice soft and low. Her black riding suit and boots were worn, even shabby, but her white shirt was spotless and her tawny hair shone bright in the sun. And though she hadn't let go of the rifle, she wasn't protecting herself from an attack from behind; his strength would have easily overwhelmed hers.

But most puzzling was her reputation for violence—at odds with her vulnerability. And the ancient rifle hanging loose now from her hand—would it even fire? That filthy weapon might just be a greater menace than the girl who held it.

"Well?" The rancor in her voice had been replaced with resignation.

"The White's Station bank was robbed this morning. Lany Mills, the old clerk there, was shot. He may die."

"Russell?"

"We heard the shots, my brother and I. We were coming into town." His hand reached for her of its own volition, but he drew it back. "I didn't want to kill him."

As her shoulders began to shake, he reached out again. She jumped away as if he'd burned her, spinning around, her face white, her green eyes spitting fire.

"Don't touch me! How dare you touch me!" She flung the rifle into the dirt, covered her face with both hands, and sank to the ground sobbing.

He stood there stolidly as she cried at his feet. The Donovan comfort was holding, touching. He didn't know what else to offer her. He crouched down beside her but made no move toward her.

Though her sobs subsided, her body continued to tremble. When he spoke her name, she raised her face, her cheeks wet with tears, her lips quivering. What he'd taken for a shadow on her jaw, he could now see was a fading bruise. She was so small. So young. He longed to stroke her bright hair, wipe the dampness from her face, hold her as he'd hold his little sister Irene when some vast grief would overcome her.

"I'm sorry, Jesse. More than I can tell you."

"I'm sure it... Russell always..." She stood, ignoring his proffered hand, and gazed out across the garden again. "I have to tell my father. But what can I say? This will kill him."

"Do you have to tell him everything?"

"Don't you think he'd realize that Russell never came home? My father may be ill, *Mister* Donovan, but he isn't an idiot!"

"No. That's not what I meant. Not at all." He stifled the impatience in his voice. "I only... maybe we could tell him there was an accident. Something like that."

She was silent for so long he began to apologize again, but she interrupted him. "Why would you do that?" He had no answer. "Would you do that?"

"If that's what you want."

"The truth will kill him, you know." A sob began, but it caught in her throat and came no further. "What can we tell him?"

"Maybe just the bare facts—that there was a holdup at the bank and Russell was killed."

"Will you do it?"

"Of course. Now?"

She stepped away, her feet dragging. As he entered the cabin behind her, Adam nearly choked on the heat of the fire that burned high in spite of the stifling day. The old man sat in a rough rocking chair, his legs covered with a faded quilt. He was bent over at the shoulders, his gray hair wild around his head, his eyes sunken deep in their sockets. For the first time since he'd drawn his gun that morning, Adam wondered if he'd had another choice.

"Daddy, this is Adam Donovan."

The old man bobbed his head several times. In a hollow, quavering voice, he said, "Wondered if the Donovans would git around to callin'."

"I'm sorry I haven't come before, sir." *I should have been here years ago.* "I'm afraid I have some bad news for you."

"Ain't nothin' but bad news in this world, boy. Ain't never been 'round here anyways." When Adam didn't speak, the old man roused himself. "Well, son, what is it?"

"It's about Russell, sir."

"Been a heap o' trouble t' me, that boy has. What's he gotten inta now?" The invalid peered at Adam as if through a fog. "He ain't in jail ag'in, is he?"

"No, sir. But there was a bank robbery in town today. The clerk got shot, and I'm sorry to tell you... Russell got shot, too."

"What's that? My boy got shot?" The old man tried to raise himself but fell back into the chair. "Who shot him? How bad's he hurt?"

"I'm afraid, sir, I have to tell you... Russell is dead."

The old man stared into the fire, his brow furrowed, his eyes blank. "Dead?" he whispered. "Dead." He wrapped his arms around his body and rocked back and forth, but made no further sound. Jesse gestured for Adam to follow her outside.

"I thank you. I couldn't have told him."

Again he wanted to gather her close and hold her while she cried her grief away. Instead, he reached for her shoulder. She twisted away before he made contact and he snapped his hand back. *I'm not some goddamned trail bum.* But anger would serve no purpose here, and he fought down his irritation.

"Please let me know if I can do anything to help you."

"There is something." She spoke so softly he had to bend to hear her. "You could bring him home."

"Of course. Tomorrow morning? Shall I bring the preacher, too?"

"Please." Her voice was breaking. "It would mean so much to Daddy."

JESSE STUMBLED INTO the cabin, stopping just inside the door. When the appaloosa's hoofbeats faded, she leaned against the wall, her strength spent. She watched her father, still rocking himself, still wrapped in his own arms, and she remembered a time when those arms had been wrapped around her. When she'd been his little girl, his baby. When he'd been even taller and stronger than the rider who'd just departed. She spoke to him but he didn't hear. She tried to share his grief.

"Damn you," she whispered, raising a fist to the spectre of her brother that hung there in the shadows. "God damn you."

Then, using the wall for balance, she forced her legs to take her to her room. She fell on the bed, trembling as the aspen leaves in a sudden wind, and curled herself into a ball. Guilt, fear, rage, and shame swept across her in rapid succession. Yet she did not cry.

As evening fell, she roused herself and willed her body to stand. She splashed water on her face, dried it with a piece of rough toweling. Putting a tentative finger on the pitcher that had been her mother's, she traced the outlines of the delicate yellow flowers, and allowed herself the luxury of a single sigh.

She went out to light the stove, grabbed a frying pan, and slung a lump of lard into it. As she chopped two scraggly scallions, she stared out the window, wishing for a stalk of celery, a carrot, anything more than the leftover beef tail from yesterday's soup and a single soft potato. Her brother hadn't brought stores home in over a week. Her brother...

Her hands fell to trembling so badly she had to drop the knife before it cut her. She grabbed the front of the sink, knuckles white, teeth clenched, knees close to buckling. A few deep, harsh breaths helped her regain some control. But the lard was burning.

She'd thought the day could not be worse. She began again: cleaned the frying pan, added the lard, the scallion. She cut the eyes out of the potato to plant in the garden, then sliced what remained. Scooped the marrow out of the bones and let it all fry together. It was little enough for two people; she put most of it on the old man's plate. Absently, she added chicory and dandelion leaves to the coffee pot. She'd let it boil while he ate.

She glanced over at him. His chin rested against his scrawny chest, spittle leaking from his mouth. His flannel shirt was patched and faded, but there were no new clothes—hadn't been new clothes for years.

She had to shake his shoulder to waken him, and he raised empty eyes to hers.

"Here's your supper." She offered the plate, but he waved carelessly and knocked it to the floor. It clattered and broke, the food spilling in a greasy trail. Silently, she mopped up the mess. It wasn't like he was going to enjoy it anyway. It wasn't like he'd been thinking of anything but his son. The son he loved like an only child. In spite of every bad thing he'd done, and everything she'd tried to do to change it. To make herself matter to him again.

After rinsing out the dirty rag, Jesse reached for a mason jar on the shelf above the sink, spilled the coins onto the table. Two dollars and thirty-nine cents.

That's it. That's all there is. And how am I going to get more? Even if I could rope a cow, I don't know where he found the strays. I don't know how to get them to town or who he sold them to. How am I going to manage...

She sank into a chair, letting the tears begin. Fat and round, they rolled single file down her cheeks. No sobs, no sniffles, no sighs. Just fat, round tears that looked at tomorrow and found no hope.

But she'd learned not to expect anything from the future. Today was to be gotten through. Yesterday was gone and they'd survived it. Tomorrow was a dream—as far away, as unreachable as the evening star. Tonight, she had to help him onto the cot that served for his bed, empty the can he used to relieve himself, and build up the fire. Then see if she could choke down some food. Even that poor substitute for coffee would be better than nothing.

Tomorrow would come or it wouldn't. It would be good or it would be bad. Tonight, there were things that had to be done. Wiping a hand across her cheek, Jesse stood and straightened her spine, and began to do the things that needed to be done.

... to be continued

Be the first to get the news!

You can sign up for my newsletter &
get a free book, as well as updates,
early notice of new releases, special promotions, & more.
OR
If you want a copy of my newest books
before they're available to the general public,
consider joining my Launch Team!
Find more information here[1]:

Acknowledgments

To my mother, Janet, and my husband, Rich, for their unwavering
support;
to the ladies of the Prose & Precision group for their thoughtful input
and suggestions;
To Justin Portelli & the Fair Lawn Writers' Circle, whose
encouragement prompted me to pursue publication;
to all of you, I offer my eternal gratitude.

A Short Glossary of Terms

IRISH TERMS:

This book encompasses a time when Irish people were forbidden to speak, read or write in their native language. Words were whispered and passed down secretly from generation to generation, and came to be spelled phonetically. "Mo chroi" became "Machree"; "mo chuisle" became "Macushla", etc. It is those spellings I've decided to use in this historical saga.

§

Bawn: fair of skin, also pretty/beautiful
Colleen: girl or young woman
Machree: my heart
Macushla: my lifeblood, also *"acushla"*
Mavourneen: beloved

§

Note: The Donovan family uses "acushla" when this endearment is directed to the males, "macushlah" for the females. This is a little quirk that, as far as I know, occurs only in my family.

About the Author

GIFFORD MACSHANE IS the author of historical novels that feature a family of Irish immigrants who settle in the Arizona Territory in the late 1800s. With an accessible literary style, MacShane draws out her characters' hidden flaws and strengths as they grapple with both physical and emotional conflicts.

Singing almost before she could talk, MacShane has always loved folk music, whether it be Irish, Appalachian, spirituals, or the songs of the cowboys. Her love of the Old West goes back to childhood, when her father introduced her to the works of Zane Grey. Later she became interested in the Irish diaspora, having realized her father's family had lived through *An Gorta Mor*, the Great Irish Potato Famine of the mid-1800s.

Writing allows her to combine her three great interests into a series of family stories with romance, folk song lyrics, and Celtic mysticism. Having grown up in a large & often boisterous Irish-American family, she is intimately acquainted with the workings of such a clan & uses those experiences to good purpose (though no names will be named!)

MacShane is a member of the Historical Novel Society. Though she loves to sing, her cats don't always appreciate it. A self-professed grammar nerd who can be caught diagramming sentences for fun, she currently lives in Pennsylvania with her husband Richard, the Pied Piper of stray cats.

What Reviewers Say

about the
DONOVAN FAMILY SAGA

§

THE WINDS OF MORNING

- Filled with characters you'll never forget, and historical facts you'll wish you could.

- In some parts this book would just tear into my very soul and other parts it touched my heart.

- Beautifully written with outstanding characters that will touch your heart and soul!

§

WHISPERS IN THE CANYON

- A heartwarming, yet gut-wrenching, romance novel. This novel is one of the most well-written and well-developed books I have read in a long time.

- A beautiful and heartfelt piece of fiction that goes beyond the simple western romance to deliver a tender, emotional and psychological tale of one woman's bravery in a time when few people really cared or appreciated such strength.

§

THE WOODSMAN'S ROSE

- The author does a fantastic job pulling you in and kept me glued to the pages right to the end.

- There is enough swoon-worthy, though tender, romance to melt even the coldest of hearts, and there is plenty of action and adventure for those who enjoy novels that keep them on the edge of their seat.

- Although the story takes place in savage times and there is an element of that savagery in it, at its heart it is a gentle tale about gentle people. Whilst the book deals with the realities of life there is a mystical element to it which runs as a distinct thread throughout.

§

RAINBOW MAN

- You will be drawn in, page by page. You will feel a part of the tale and you will want there to be a happy ending. Brilliant read.

- The story and characters that are so well written I caught myself talking, crying, laughing and yelling at them!

- A wonderfully descriptive period novel with a gorgeous hero and a frustratingly naive and clueless heroine.

§

WITHOUT THE THUNDER

- A page turner and hard to put down.

- Brings drama, anxiety and fear along with the prejudice and hate. The story moves fluidly with descriptive scenes and multiple storylines.